Nude Sleeping in a Hammock

A Novel

Gary Rinehart

ISBN-10: 0615645941
EAN-13: 9780615645940

PROLOGUE

By age 65 John Hayden's religious faith had waned. But over the next ten years inexplicable coincidences restored his belief in divine intervention. They all involved her-the *nude sleeping in a hammock*.

At her birth in Florence she was named "Sweet Dreams". In 1915 she was sent to the Panama Pacific International Exhibition in San Francisco.

Purchased there and taken to Piedmont, she was named "Eva". In the year 2000 John Hayden sent Eva away. He wondered why bad luck followed.

It was many years earlier when John took his family to Hawaii. During their tour of the volcano their son Jeffrey grabbed a piece of lava, hoping to add it to his collectibles at home. When the guide told how Madame Pele would bring ten years of bad luck to anyone removing her lava, Jeffrey ran back to deposit the rock where he found it.

John came to believe that Eva was like Madame Pele.

CHAPTER ONE

In October of 2009 John Hayden was scheduled to play piano at the Piedmont Jazz Festival. Graham Carter, publisher of the Weekly Piedmont Courier, recommended John's playing to the committee in charge of the event. Graham was a reporter with the Oakland Tribune when, twenty years earlier, he visited John's law office to question him about his recent trial. There he discovered that John had been a jazz pianist before he became a lawyer.

Not knowing that John was undergoing a bout with depression, Graham sent the Courier reporter, a young lady named Robin, to interview John at his home on Wildwood Avenue.

Sarah, John's wife, escorted Robin out to the patio where she and John could sit under the umbrella. John tried to be on his best behavior. Robin's questions began:

"When did you start with the piano?"

"At age nine my mother took me to see a movie called 'A Song to Remember.' It was about the life of Chopin. Then all I wanted to do was to play Chopin. When I was a kid, movies were important. You young people don't understand that."

"So you started with classical music?"

"Yes- lessons with a kind old teacher. At age eleven, I played the Chopin Polonaise at a school assembly."

"How did you get interested in jazz?"

"I was about twelve. Sherman Clay in downtown Oakland allowed kids to listen to records. That's when I heard Art Tatum and Teddy Wilson. So then, I wanted to play jazz. You young people don't know about jazz. All you know is the Grateful Dead."

Robin thought: *Why is he so cranky. I thought jazz musicians were supposed to be happy.* She answered:

"Oh no. I just graduated from NYU. We heard a lot of jazz there. But, tell me, how long have you lived in Piedmont?"

John thought: *Why is she looking at the wisteria? Did someone tell her that's where Eva used to be?* He answered:

"You said 'I just graduated from NYU??' Why is it that you young people end a sentence by raising your voice, as if you were asking a question? You all do that! To answer your question: My parents moved here in 1951. In 1972 they moved to a house in Oakland above the Caldecott Tunnel. They lost that house in the Oakland hills fire. In1964 we bought a house on Harvard Road. We bought this house on Wildwood in 1968."

Trying to lighten the atmosphere, Robin asked:

"On my way in I noticed that beautiful grand piano in your living room. I've never seen anything like it. Is it an antique?"

"Yes-It's a Steinway concert grand. It left the Steinway factory in 1871. We had it restored by the best Steinway technician-he was then."

"What was his name?"

"Sheldon Smith. He's dead now. A lot of my friends are. Maybe I shouldn't be around either."

"Did you play piano, like, professionally?"

"That's another one. Where would you and your friends be without the word "like"? What is it? An adjective? Adverb? Preposition? You probably don't know, but I did play, like, professionally."

Robin thought: *This guy's an ass. I'll try to ignore that and get through with this.* She asked:

"When was that?"

"My first gig was after I graduated from high school. I played at a summer resort- six nights a week. I had to work as a kid. You young people wouldn't understand that either."

"Then did you go to college?"

"Not then. I wanted to major in music and then go on to law school. But the draft for the Korean War was still on. You don't know about that. I'd be eligible for the GI Bill if I went in right away. If I waited it would expire. I heard about the Navy music program-four years with one at the Music School in Washington, D.C. I passed the audition and got through the school. Then they sent me to the Sixth Fleet Band in the Mediterranean. So four years later I had the GI Bill for college."

"Were you on a ship?"

"Most of the time we were on a ship named the *Salem*. There we had to sleep in close quarters. In the old days sailors had to sleep on hammocks. They'd stay level as the ship rolled."

"Did you play much jazz with the Navy Band?"

"Jazz was our hobby, but we usually had to play other things-military music, concert things, big band and small combo arrangements. But in our spare time we played jazz. In every port, someone would invite us to sit in at a local jazz club, usually some smoky bar with an out-of-tune upright piano and a drum set. When we were in our home port at Villefranche, in France, we played jazz almost every night at the Hot Club in Nice. I was lucky to be with good players like Gene Martinelli on tenor sax, Cruz Santos on trombone and Roscoe James on drums."

"Did you ever meet up with those friends after the Navy?"

John thought: *That reunion trip was before I sold Eva, when we could still enjoy things like that.* He answered:

"Yes. We had a reunion in Washington DC about ten years ago."

"Did you ever play with someone famous?"

"When our ship was in Istanbul, Dizzy Gillespie was on a good-will tour. Cruz Santos had the nerve to go to Dizzy's hotel room to ask him to come play with us at the USO that night. He did it. He brought one of his new members, a young man named Quincy Jones. We played a *B flat blues* and *I'll Remember April*. Dizzy was marvelous. The USO was filled with service men who looked up to Dizzy as the hero he was.

Here's a photo that was in the Turkish newspaper. It doesn't show me-I was off to the side on an upright piano. It does show Gene-next to the Chief on the stage behind Dizzy."

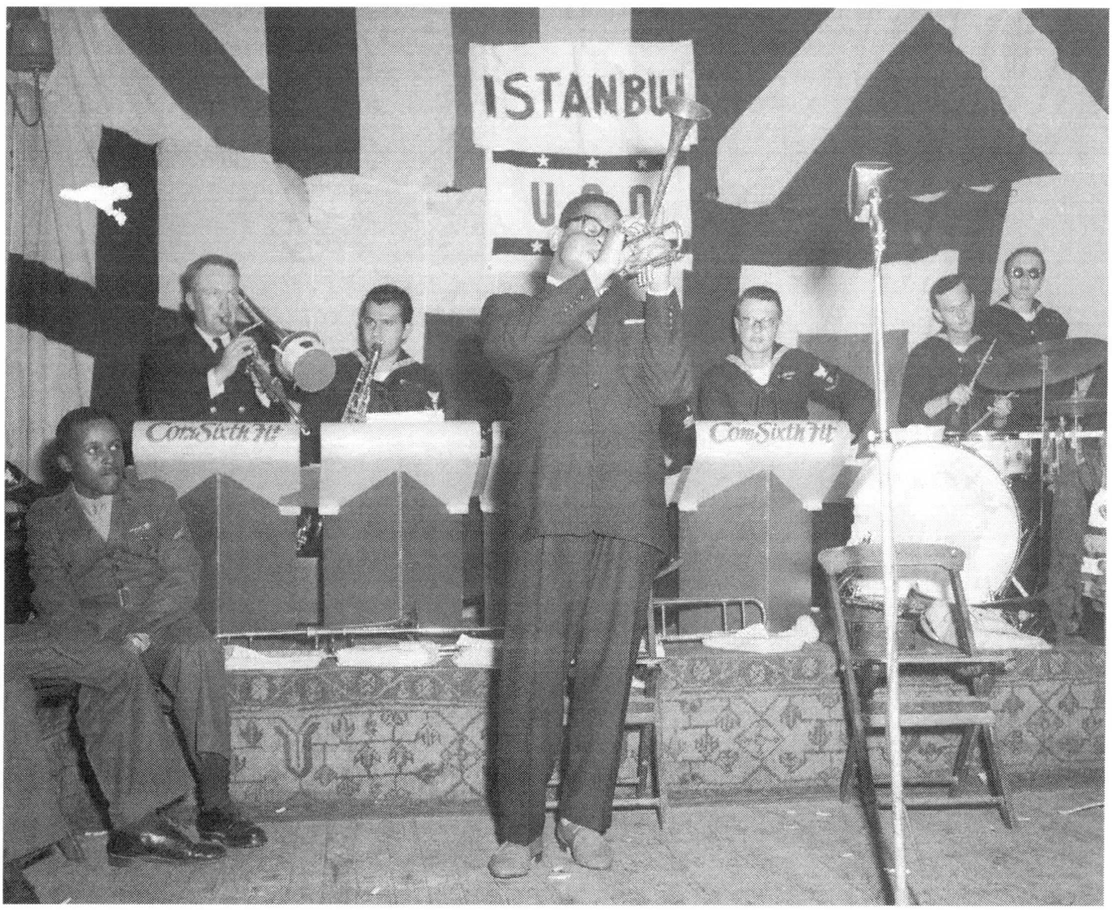
ISTANBUL
U S O
ComSixthFlt
ComSixthFlt

"Tell me about your college years".

"I wanted to go to Cal Berkeley. In the Navy-while at sea-I took correspondence courses from UC Extension. Since our home-port was Villefranche most of the courses were in French. But at UC I didn't major in French. My father was a CPA, so I majored in accounting, just to be sure of having a job. You young people never had to worry about getting a job-we did. But I always wanted to be a lawyer, so I tried to get the grades needed to get into law school."

"When did you meet Sarah?"

"Just back from the Navy I went with my mother to Corpus Christi church. After mass, walking to the car, my mother said, 'There's Sarah Riley. You know our friends Al and Dorothy-she's their daughter.' Sarah stopped her car. I saw that classic face, the kind I'd seen on statues in Italy. Two years later-January 30th, 1960- we were married -at Corpus Christi."

"So you were still in school after you were married?"

"Sure. Sarah worked to put me through. Her salary and the GI Bill made me a lawyer. When Gregory and Jeffrey came along, she was a full time Mom."

"How did you decide what field of law you wanted to go into?"

"At a reception for the first year students Dean Prosser asked me what kind of a lawyer I'd like to be. I told him I'd like to be involved with international law and civil rights. With that look of disdain he said I'd likely take the first opportunity to come along, and it would not be in international law or civil rights. During my third year Sarah delivered Gregory and the GI Bill ran out. When I graduated in 1963 I was offered a job with the State. I snapped at it. The Dean was right."

"And what was that job?"

"I handled eminent domain cases-where rights-of-way were required for highway projects. When property owners wouldn't agree on compensation, we filed suit to have a jury decide. Then I went into private practice doing the same thing."

"What about your family now?"

"We have two grown sons. They both went through the Piedmont schools. Gregory is married and lives in Piedmont with his wife Michelle and their two daughters. He's a real estate appraiser. He has the 'Appraisal Institute' designation-quite an accomplishment.

Ever since high school he has rowed crew. He still finds time to do it. I hope to see him in the Olympics."

"And your other son?"

"Jeffrey is married. He and his wife Kathleen also have two daughters. He's a computer expert. He's very active in his church. I think he's on his way to becoming a minister. He studies theology and all that. He just moved his family to Coeur d'Alene, Idaho. We miss them a lot."

Robin thought: *He's not so much an ass when he talks about his family and career. Everything else seems to bother him.* She asked:

"Did Sarah help you with your career?"

"Oh, yes. A lawyer needs to make contact with the public. Sarah did that for me. She joined the Lawyer's wives and became President of that. She joined the Oakland Symphony Guild and became President of that. She joined a branch of Children's Hospital. She gave a lot of parties. She even found time to do all the bookkeeping for my office."

"So now are you retired?"

John thought: *She would have to ask that! After Eva I've been out of work-not retired, damn it!* He answered:

"More or less".

"What are you doing with music now?"

"Classical and the standards. I love the romantics like Chopin and Rachmaninoff and the impressionists like Debussy and Ravel. I spend a lot of time with the standards. And, I love the musical theatre, especially Andrew Lloyd Webber. We saw Phantom in San Francisco and in New York."

Robin folded her tablet. She hoped it didn't show, but she thought something didn't ring true about John. *What's bothering him? Why that "you young people" routine? Why is he "more or less" retired? Why does he think he should be dead? Why that slow and stumbling speech? He criticizes me for saying "like". What nerve-he mispronounces half his words. What about his poor wife? There's some friction there.*

All during the interview, Robin noticed the semi-circle archway covered with wisteria at the rear of the garden. It covered nothing. She thought there should be something under that archway. *Could it be a grave? With this guy who knows?*

John saw Robin to the door. *Why am I doing this?* He thought. *That damn arthritis may prevent me from playing at all. Sarah will never agree to sell that damn house. She's been crying ever since we sold Eva.*

Looking from the kitchen out to the garden where Eva had been reminded Sarah of how disappointed she was with John. She thought: *If he hadn't sold her we'd still be happy. Where is she? In some glitzy Las Vegas Hotel? That statue! That statue! I've got to stop thinking about it.*

CHAPTER TWO

In the nineteenth century piano makers from Europe came to the United States. 1n 1850 Heinrich Steinweg came from Germany to New York. There he changed his name to Henry Steinway. Over the next forty years, he and his sons virtually invented the modern concert grand piano. Steinway became the piano preferred by the artists like Anton Rubinstein, Ignace Paderewski and Sergei Rachmaninoff. In1839 William Knabe, also from Germany, began building pianos in Baltimore. His pianos were preferred in the southern states.

In Italy, the nineteenth century was good to a sculptor named Antonio Frilli. In 1860 he opened his gallery at 4 Via Dei Fossi, Florence. There he and his students carved statues in Carrara marble. Carrara, a city in Tuscany, was famous for the white and gray marble used by sculptors since the time of Ancient Rome. Michelangelo carved his David into this precious stone.

Frilli refused to bow to the trend toward modesty. He kept the Greek and Italian tradition of realistically depicting the human body. Artists and composers had always bucked popular trends, but never so much as in the late nineteenth century. In France, the impressionists were not deterred by the establishment. They were painters like Monet, Cézanne and Gauguin, and they were composers like Debussy, Ravel and Satie. In America, despite its social stigma, jazz was taking hold.

Frilli carved his vision of a maiden. Her shapely body slept in a hammock-nude. With her right arm hanging down to clutch a dropped handkerchief, her legs crossed, her middle discreetly covered by a shawl, her bare breasts erect and her classic face to one side she seemed to be waiting to be awakened by her lover's kiss. The hammock's rounded stanchions, topped by the rings from which it hung, were delicately carved as they arose from the solid marble base. Frilli's hammock was like those that allowed sailors to sleep through heavy seas. Its underside of tightly braided strands spread ever so slightly under the pleasant weight of the maiden's body. As if to tolerate the heat of the day the maiden had discarded two blankets-- one casually thrown under her feet, the other under her head.

In 1893 Antonin Dvorak left his home in Czechoslovakia to visit the United States, there to compose his Symphony No. 9, *From the New World*. In 1894 Antonio Frilli named his nude sleeping maiden *Sweet Dreams*. Would she too visit the New World? She remained in Florence when Antonio's death came in 1896.

CHAPTER THREE

In 1904 Reuben Hale, owner of Hale's Department store on Market Street in San Francisco, proposed to his fellow merchants that they host an exposition in honor of the opening of the Panama Canal. After all, America had taken over the task of building it. Ferdinand de Lesseps of France had tried to employ the same sea level plan he had in building the Suez Canal. Three years of that ended in disaster. America would do the job right. The press called the Panama project "The thirteenth Labor of Hercules." The American design would use locks to allow the waterway to rise into a lake in the mountains and descend again to the sea. So why not a celebration in America? What better place than San Francisco---*The Jewel of the West, The Paris of the Pacific*?

Hale got his answer. To the other merchants his suggestion seemed as preposterous as the notion by the lunatic they called *Emperor Norton* that a bridge could be built across the San Francisco bay.

Two years later, at 5:12 AM on April 18, 1906, San Francisco suffered its earthquake- the nation's greatest urban disaster. The tremor and the fire it spawned was the equivalent of 400 Hiroshima atomic bombs. Three thousand people were killed. With temperatures exceeding 2,000 degrees, the fire melted glass and twisted steel. An area of 508 city blocks was leveled. More than 28,000 structures were destroyed.

News of the quake was most poignant in Italy. It had awakened the great Enrico Caruso as he slept at San Francisco's Palace Hotel. Caruso returned to Italy unscathed, but now Italians would eye San Francisco with suspicion.

Over the next few years, San Franciscans took heroic steps to rise from the ashes. Hale again advanced his idea. This time it fell upon willing ears. By hosting a World's Fair superior to the one in St. Louis in 1904 San Francisco could prove that it was alive and well. The fair would be named *The Panama Pacific International Exposition*, abbreviated as *the PPIE*. A company was formed to receive money from the federal and state governments and from subscriptions sold to the public. Renowned architects were hired to design the buildings. *The Palace of fine Arts*, by Bernard Maybeck, was in the group of eight buildings to be crowned by *The Tower of Jewels*. It remains today as a San Francisco landmark.

The Panama Canal was to open in 1914. What a timely celebration the PPIE would be! Artists the world over, including the Frilli Gallery, were invited to display their works.

The Exposition began on February 20, 1915. In the White House President Wilson pushed a key sending the wireless message to San Francisco that unleashed water cascading around the figure of Hercules towering over the Panama Canal. Biplanes circled over the Tower of Jewels. Among the cheering crowd were scions of industry, Thomas Edison and Henry Ford among them, there to promote their accomplishments.

Artists from around the world graced the PPIE. In attendance was the French composer Camille Saint Saens, who led the symphony orchestra in "Hail to California", his composition for the occasion. But the orchestra was not the San Francisco Symphony. Although that association of local musicians had completed four successful seasons, the PPIE organizers thought that a better-known American orchestra should be featured at this world's fair. They chose the Boston Symphony. Ignace Paderewski played Chopin's Polonaise at an ornate Steinway concert grand. For some lighter entertainment one hundred beauties came from Zeigfeld's follies to dance around the festivities.

World War1 had begun in Europe. Paderewski told the crowd in San Francisco how his beloved Poland was suffering. Because of alliances and conflicts over many years, Austria, Hungary and Germany became embroiled in war against Russia, France and

Great Britain. In 1915, and until its entry into the conflict in 1917, the United States remained neutral. Italy had a treaty of alliance with Austria-Hungary, but it refused to enter the war on its assertion that its allies had started a war of aggression. Although Italy entered the war against its former allies in 1915, the Frilli Gallery had already sent statues to San Francisco, along with a booklet containing their photos, the largest of which portrayed the sleeping nude maiden-Antonio Frill's *Sweet Dreams*. She would be displayed in the Italian Pavilion, Palace of Manufactures.

The Panama Pacific International Exposition was a great success. By its close on December 4, 1915, the Frilli Gallery had sold all its displayed statues, including *Sweet Dreams,* the *nude sleeping in a hammock.*

P. P. I. E.
San Francisco

Italian Pavilion
Palace of Manufactures

ANTONIO FRILLI

Established 1860

MARBLE STATUARY
INTERIOR & GARDEN DECORATIONS
LIGHTING FIXTURES

Largest Exporters of MARBLE
In the World

Member of International Jury of Awards. P.P.I.E.

4 Via Dei Fossi- Florence, Italy

INTRODUCTORY

Among the prominent foreign firms exhibiting at the Panama-Pacific International Exposition at San Francisco is the firm of Antonio Frilli of Florence, Italy, the largest and oldest exporter of marble statuary in Italy. This firm has on exhibition some 1500 pieces of statuary of various sizes and marbles and the purpose of this catalog is to give concisely an idea of the beauty of this work.

The photographs reproduced herein can convey but an inadequaté idea of the magnitude and magnificence of this display—it must be seen to be appreciated. A hearty invitation is extended to all to visit these exhibits in the Italian Pavilion and the Manufacturers Building and inspect this work. An attendant will cheerfully show you through the exhibits and describe the work in detail.

It will give us pleasure to entertain you.

ANTONIO FRILLI
ITALY'S
OLDEST AND LARGEST EXPORTER OF
MARBLE STATUARY

Established 1860

Main Office and Show Room
Florence, Italy
4 via dei Fossi

Special Display
Palace of Manufactures and Italian Pavilion
P. P. I. E.
San Francisco, Cal.

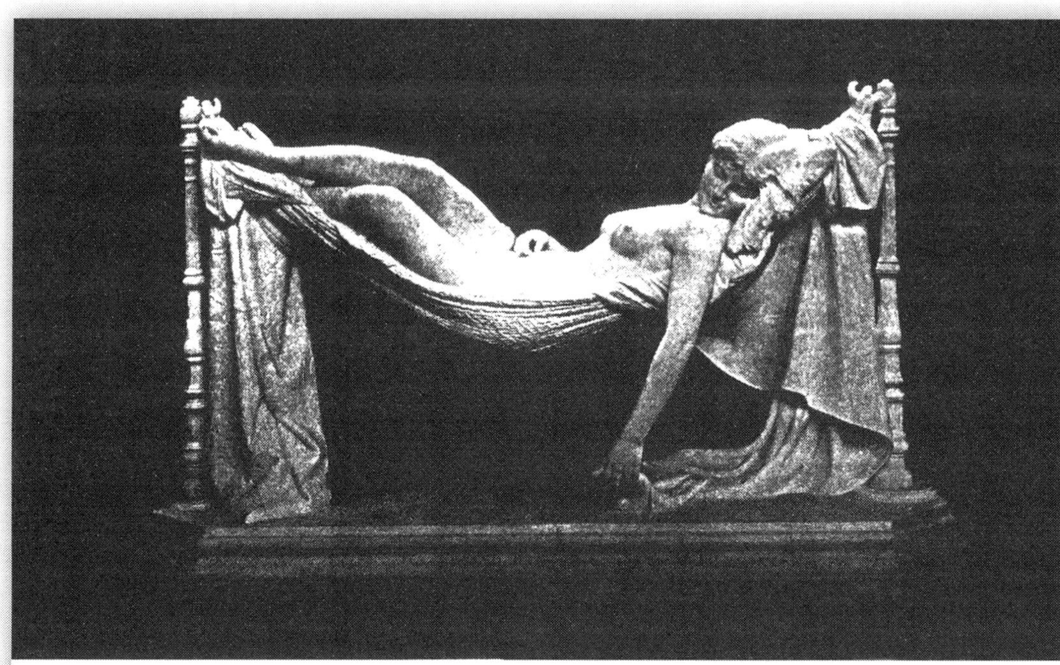

SWEET DREAMS *designed by* PROF. ALBANO
executed by A. FRILLI

Carrara Marble. Life Size Statue

CHAPTER FOUR

Piemonte, a region of Italy, means "foot of the mountain". It ascends into the Alps as it traverses easterly from its neighbor, Liguria, lying on the shores of the Mediterranean.

Named after her Italian sister, Piedmont is a city ascending into the hills as it traverses easterly from its neighbor, Oakland, lying on the shores of the San Francisco Bay. Occupied by farms in 1870, by1890 families from San Francisco and Oakland were moving into the Piedmont hills. As the twentieth century began, Piedmont became a separate municipality. After the earthquake and fire, many San Franciscans moved to the east bay, some to Piedmont.

Although William and Walter Blair had followed the Gold Rush to California, they had more success in land speculation. They bought a track in Piedmont from the federal government for the exorbitant sum of $1.25 per acre. Their idea was to bring people up the hill by cable cars to their *Piedmont Land Company*. Although they eventually scrapped the cable car idea, they did build a rail line from Oakland ending at what they named Piedmont Park. There they built a grand hotel with a large area for the display of art and sculpture from Europe.

Frank C. Havens was a real estate developer who had the financial backing of the very wealthy Francis Marion "Borax" Smith. Smith was a mining and real estate tycoon who successfully extracted borax from Death Valley and the Nevada desert. His project was the creation of a rail transit in the east bay he named the *The Key System*. Haven's project was the hotel he was building in the Oakland-Berkeley hills he named *The Claremont*. As a side, Havens bought a few tracks of land from Blair's Piedmont Land Company. He then took it upon himself to name the streets. One was Wildwood Avenue.

As a lover of art and music, Havens was a member of the Bohemian Club of San Francisco. Among the artists, musicians and authors he welcomed to his Piedmont home on Hazel Lane were Joaquin Miller, *the poet of the Sierras*, and Jack London. By 1908, Havens planned to build another Piedmont mansion for himself. He reserved a large parcel adjacent to the upper portion of Wildwood Avenue. Because his wife was fascinated by things oriental, he built a replica of a Rajah's castle. Huge teakwood beams and several Hindu craftsmen were brought from India. Japanese and Chinese workers, encamped on the property for two years, worked on the structure. In paneled walls were niches for hand-carved Buddha's. Of course, the mansion had to have an opium den. Around the estate, Havens built a thick concrete wall topped by a decorative wrought iron fence. The rear wall marked Wildwood Avenue.

Gerald Patrick Keeley was also in the Bohemian Club. He loved all the arts, but his fascination was with marble sculptures. While architects known as the Newsom Brothers were designing his new home at Wildwood Avenue, Keeley took advantage of the Panama Pacific Exposition to shop for garden statues. There he found the answer to his dreams: The patina of the Carrara marble felt smooth as Keeley's hand caressed a life-sized maiden lying nude in a hammock. On the base of the statue was carved "Frilli, Firenzi". The purchase was made. *Sweet Dreams*, having been born in Florence, would move from San Francisco to Wildwood Avenue in Piedmont. Discretion would place the nude maiden in the rear garden. For the garden at the entrance to his home Keeley chose another Frilli creation-a Roman Bath surrounded by cherubs.

Remaining today is Piedmont's breathtaking view of the San Francisco Bay. Mount Tamalpais can be seen in all her splendor. According to the Indian legend, Tamalpais, like the nude maiden of "Sweet Drams", was a sleeping lady waiting to be awakened by her lover's kiss.

Chapter Five

In 1962, while John Hayden was in his third year of law school, his wife Sarah delivered their first son. They named him Gregory. As Greg was the first grandchild for John and Sarah's parents, he became a star attraction.

John was twenty eight when, in 1964, he was admitted to practice law in California. In that year he became employed as an attorney by the State of California.

In 1965 another son, Jeffrey, was welcomed into the family. Greg and Jeff were both healthy and active. Thanks to Sarah, the family at home did quite well while John attended to the law business.

Also in 1965 John and Sarah bought their first home on Harvard Road in Piedmont. To afford the $25,000 they borrowed $5,000 from Sarah's grandfather and $20,000 from the bank on a GI loan. Sarah agreed that John should have a piano. They bought a new Baldwin baby grand for $3,200, payable on time over three years.

In 1968 John was asked to join a law firm in Martinez. He jumped at the opportunity to leave the state office and go into private practice. One morning, while waiting in court for his case to be called, John talked to a law school friend who had become a divorce specialist. He told John that his divorce client wanted to sell an old grand piano. John and Sarah went to see the only remaining piece of furniture of what had been a happy home. It was ugly. It was old. It was unplayable. It had large chips in its rosewood case that had been painted black. But it was a concert grand. And, it was a Steinway.

John telephoned Sherman Clay, the Steinway dealer in Oakland.

"Will you tell me the name and phone number of the man you hire to restore old Steinways?"

"His name is Sheldon Smith. I don't know his number. He lives somewhere on the Peninsula-you can look it up."

Sheldon inspected the piano. Checking the serial number with the Steinway records, he determined that it left the factory in New York in 1871. He told John that since he would work on it in his spare time it would take three years, perhaps more. For $3,600 it would be a complete re-build, including a new sound board and the restoration of the rosewood case with its hand carving. John thought that in three years he could sell the Baldwin for that amount-it would be paid for by then. He bought the old Steinway for the asking price of $150 and had it moved to Sheldon's shop in San Francisco.

Also in 1968 John and Sarah sold their home on Harvard Road for $30,000 and bought their home on Wildwood Avenue for $55,000. The house was built in 1923 for Lester White, a prominent attorney in Oakland. It was designed by architects Sidney and Noble Newsom. After White's death, his executor put the house on the market. John and Sarah became its second owners.

The house resembled a Tuscan villa, tile roof and all. Extending from the opening in the wall and wrought iron fence along Wildwood, the concrete driveway resembled flagstones. Directly ahead were the garage doors. To the left was the gate to the side yard. To the right was the entry to the front door. A garden occupied the rest of the frontage.

The stucco on the exterior of the house was molded into a wave-like surface in the style of the California missions. The exterior doors, two and one-half inches thick, bore black iron hardware. Two sets of double garage doors swung outward. Like the front door, they were covered by a pattern of decorative nails set in a metal circle carved into a flower. The doors' wooden panels had a smooth patina in an unidentifiable antique color. At their center were iron ring pulls resembling those on European cathedrals.

Inside, the lath and plaster walls over hardwood floors had the same wave-like texture. The interior doors, also with ring pulls, were covered by hand-carved Moorish designs. The entry hall led to the living room on the right, to the dining room straight ahead and to the ground floor hallway on the left. The staircase ascended from the entry hall to the bedrooms upstairs.

The living room measured twenty five by seventeen feet. Its plastered ceiling was divided by five 8" by 12" hewed beams. It had four sets of French doors that pulled open by iron cabin hooks. The two on the street side opened over wrought iron balconies. The two on the garden side opened onto the covered patio. The fireplace was encased in a hand-carved wooden surround over a base of Italian marble. Over the mantel was a fresco-- a painting on plaster over wood. It appeared to be a Renaissance scene at a castle overlooking a lake. The real estate agent told Sarah that the Whites had gone to Italy to get the fireplace frame and painting.

The dining room was large enough to accommodate twenty guests. It had two sets of French doors, one leading to the covered patio and one overlooking the rear garden. The inside door at the rear of the dining room swung into the butler's pantry with its sink and ceiling-high cabinets. Beyond the butler's pantry was the kitchen and laundry.

The kitchen had been designed for a maid. Adjacent to it was a bedroom- *the maid's room*- with a closet and full bath. The other bathroom downstairs, with its transom-covered doorway and its rosette-centered ceiling fixture, was off the entry hall. It was reserved for guests. The large family room off the entry hall had a floor of Mexican tiles.

The covered patio adjacent to the living and dining rooms led to the rear garden through three openings arched and rounded like pillars in a Moorish castle.

Upstairs were two large suites. All doors opened with octagonal carved glass knobs. The large guest bedroom had a closet and an adjacent full bath. French doors on its street side swung out over a Romeo and Juliette type balcony built over a stucco-covered teardrop over and between the two sets of double garage doors.

In the master suite was the bedroom with a fireplace, a library, an exterior balcony, a hallway, a full bath, a dressing table, closets and a separate half bath.

John and Sarah took the master suite, so the boys had to choose between the guest bedroom upstairs and the maid's room downstairs. They each wanted the maid's room. It had the back door and was farther from Mom and Dad. Gregory won out.

Although their parents thought they were foolish to spend that much on a house John and Sarah thought it was worth $55,000. But, they had a lot to do. Parts of the roof leaked and the kitchen needed remodeling.

Looking at the rear garden from the living room and patio, something seemed to be missing. Beyond the archways of the covered patio was a flagstone patio at ground level. Beyond that was the rear garden that extended 75 feet to a concrete wall at the back of the lot. Something was needed back there. They planted a row of pepper trees. That helped. Still, something was needed. They bought a concrete bench and put an archway of wisteria over it. That helped. Still, something was missing.

Chapter Six

As new-comers on Wildwood Avenue John and Sarah felt a bit out of place. That is, until they met their neighbors next door. Doctor William and Mary Connolly had lived there for many years.

The Connolly home was also designed by Sidney and Noble Newsom. Behind the wrought iron fence and within its front lawn was a hand-carved Roman Bath.

John and Sarah became friends with the Connollys. On a summer evening in1969, Mary Connolly invited them to a barbecue honoring the third anniversary of her son Jim's ordination to the priesthood. Connolly's barbecue was an outdoor brick fireplace and oven. John stood close by the fire, talking to Jim and his brother, Albert.

"I really like that fountain in front of your house. Where did you get that?" John asked.

Jim smiled: "It came with the house. They told us that the first owner, a guy named Keeley, bought it at the1915 Panama Exhibit in San Francisco."

"I think I heard something about that. What was that Panama thing?" John asked.

"A fair in San Francisco they named Panama because of the Panama Canal." Albert answered. "You know the Palace of Fine

Arts over there by the Marina? They say that was designed by Maybeck for that fair."

"We have an old lady in the Parish who talks about it," Jim said. "But she's a bit confused. She thinks it had something to do with Hale's Department store."

"If you like that fountain," Albert jibed, "wait till you see what's on the other side of that wall."

The Connolly house had two back yards: one by the patio off the living room, the other behind a concrete wall. Jim and Albert escorted John through the gate in the wall to come into the rear yard. There she was- a life-sized statue: *The nude sleeping in a hammock*.

"Where did you get that?" John asked.

"The same story", Jim said. "Keeley bought her at that Panama thing. We call her Eva. One time Dad and his cronies had a bit to drink. Dad took them out here at night and slapped her leg. He said, 'Go home Eva, you're drunk again.' Dad's friends believed that a neighbor named Eva gets drunk and sleeps in his hammock."

"And remember that St. Patrick's day when he painted her boobies green?" Albert asked. Jim smiled.

"We don't know how that missing piece happened". Jim said. "See, there by her feet where part of the support is gone."

John left that night thinking *what great people! And what a story about that statue and the Panama thing!*

Chapter Seven

Sheldon Smith was the technician famous pianists demanded. Whether they played classical or jazz, well-known artists insisted on his help with the instrument. On John Hayden's old Steinway Sheldon performed his miracles. A Steinway invention after the birth of John's piano was called the "Capo d'Astro".Steinway cast this bar into their plates, as the termination point for the upper tenor and treble strings, which added brilliance and color to the melody section. So as not to re-design its plates Bosendorfer followed Steinway's lead by placing its bar over the upper strings. To place a Bosendorfer-type capo on older pianos was considered impossible. Sheldon did just that on John's Steinway. He used the finest quality parts available – hammers, strings, and damper felt from Germany. The piano's "tone" comes from its soundboard. Most restorations require repairs of the original soundboards called "shims". But for John's piano Sheldon made a new sound board, using the air-dried rare spruce he had collected and stored. To create the magical curvature of the sound board was a skill Sheldon shared with few others.

In 1971 Sheldon finished the restoration. His carefully selected piano movers brought his creation from his shop in San Francisco to John's home on Wildwood Avenue in Piedmont. The Steinway concert grand, with its hand-carved rosewood case, looked as if it belonged in that large living room.

John began to play: The *Nocturne in E flat* by Chopin and *Embraceable You* by Gershwin. The piano was magnificent.

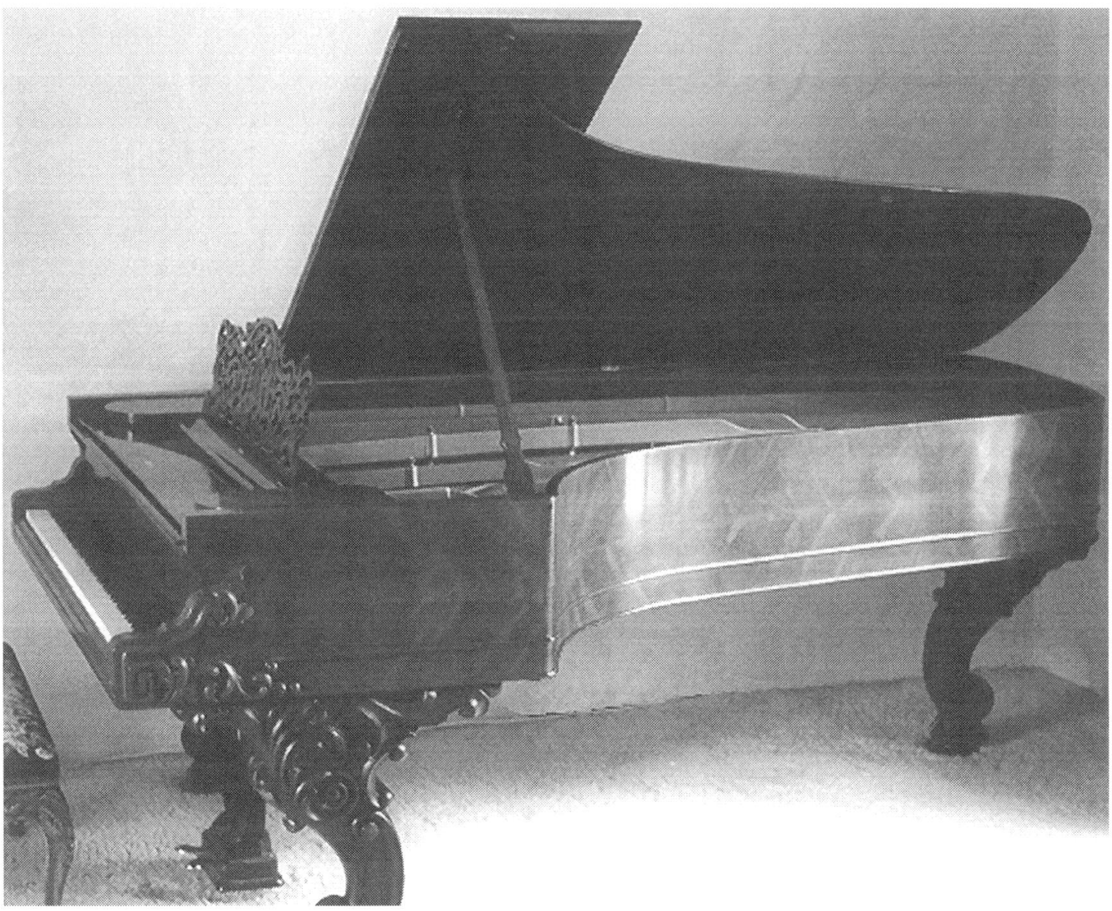

CHAPTER EIGHT

In 1972 John left the law firm in Martinez to start his own practice in Oakland. The happiness John and Sarah enjoyed in their Wildwood home, the ability of their boys to walk to Piedmont's fine schools, and, yes, even John's love for his Steinway enriched their lives. John's success as a lawyer continued its upward expansion.

In 1976 John and Sarah grieved over Dr. Connolly's death. Albert was the executor. He sold the house to Ralph and June Hogan.

Ralph Hogan was an architect and real property developer. As June had a fond childhood memory of large old homes, she fell in love with the house. Ralph bought it for her.

The Hogans became John and Sarah's friends. The first thing John noticed in their home was an old upright piano.

"It was my mother's." Ralph said. "It's an old Knabe with a player called the Ampico."

"My first piano teacher had one just like it." John said. "That Ampico player was something special-it was like the one named Duo Art. They could duplicate the expression. Other players couldn't do that. Duo Art went into Steinways. Ampicos went into Knabes."

As the years passed friendship with the Hogans grew. John and Sarah believed their luck in having good neighbors next door was providential.

CHAPTER NINE

In May, 1988 John's was offered a week's stay at a client's house at Lake Tahoe. It was a good vacation for John and Sarah. *Just for curiosity*, as he told Sarah, John contacted a realtor to *test the market* for second homes. Connie McLain gave them quite a tour. First, she showed them homes with beach frontage. They were too expensive. Then she brought them to a house one block above the lake.

It was different from their home in Piedmont-redwood siding, not stucco; shake roof, not tile; four bedrooms, not three. Downstairs, beyond the double car garage, was a recreation room with a pool table, entertainment center and an adjacent full bath. Upstairs and behind the house was a deck with benches and a sunken hot tub. Except for the three guest bedrooms and hallway, all space was open under a high beam ceiling. The dining room and bar area were to the right of the stone-floored entry hall. To the left was the living room. Spacious enough for a concert grand piano, it had a large stone fireplace. The kitchen was equipped with a refrigerator-freezer, an electric stove and oven, and a double sink with instant hot and disposal. That area with its breakfast nook was behind a brick half wall under the arched beams. In the master suite were closets with sliding doors, two sinks and a separate full bath. Like the living and dining rooms, the master suite opened onto the deck through glass sliding doors.

John and Sarah loved that Tahoe house. They thought it could be a family gathering place. With enough space, enough bedrooms and baths and in this world-renowned vacation area their sons and their families could call it home. For this "second home" they paid $250,000-nearly five times what they paid for their home in Piedmont. Of course John wanted to have a grand piano up there. He contacted his friend Sheldon Smith. Sheldon had restored a Knabe concert grand for clients who later decided to part their ways. Sarah agreed that John should buy it.

In the same year the Hogans decided to move to a smaller home for Ralph's retirement'. They agreed to sell the home to George and Betty Anderson.

Sarah was shopping for furniture for her house at Tahoe when time came for June and Ralph to move. June offered Sarah a few items, and then more: A living room coffee table, 2 antique wing-back chairs, a china cabinet, a couch, another chair for the bedroom, and then-

John answered the phone. It was June.

"John, Ralph is wondering if you could use his mother's old piano." June asked. "We don't want to move it to where we're going."

"Oh, that's so nice of you and Ralph." John answered. "We could take it to our Tahoe house. It would be perfect in the rec room downstairs by the pool table. If Ralph ever wants it we'll get it right back to him."

"He won't. He wants you to have it. And, John, you know that old statue in our back yard. The Andersons don't want it. Do you think you and Sarah would like it for your yard?"

John felt faint. He thought of the Connollys:

They told us she was from that Panama thing in San Francisco.... We call her Eva...Dad slapped her on the leg....He painted her boobies green...

"Oh June", John said, "how wonderful of you! We'll put her under the wisteria archway. We'd love to have her."

John hired movers recommended by Sheldon to take the Knabe grand, the Knabe Ampico and the other gifts from the Hogans to Tahoe. He gave them another task- to bring the statue to the Hayden home next door. As Eva seemed happy under the wisteria, no longer was anything missing back there.

CHAPTER TEN

A few months after Eva took her place under the wisteria, John hired a young attorney to help with the workload. Ted Schaefer, with two years' experience in a large firm, asked John for the opportunity.

John thought that, after all the years of doing everything himself, he could assign the routine pretrial court appearances to Ted. By saving that time, and the time in driving to courts like those in San Jose, Stockton and Martinez, John would have more time to spend at the new house at Tahoe.

Ted suggested that the firm should have a website. John reluctantly agreed. Ted hired his friend Jim Browning as the "webmaster." First, Browning asked for CVs from the two lawyers. Then he asked John:

"Tell me about this building."

"Yes." John answered. "This Breuner Building is on the list of national historical monuments. It was designed by Bernard Maybeck for the Breuner Furniture Company."

"What about your staff?

"Joyce, my secretary, is very skilled. She's mastered the procedural tasks in Eminent Domain. Her husband is a Navy flier. I hope she'll stay with me for a long time."

"You CV tells me you spent four years with the State and then four years with the firm in Martinez. Did you get some valuable experience during those years?"

"I certainly did. With the State the senior trial attorney was Jack Richards. Being with him gave me great trial experience. Then, in Martinez I was trained by Jim Noonan, another master trial lawyer. I hope I can give similar training to Ted."

"I see some cases listed here. Can you tell me about some of them?"

"Well, this first one was for a marine friend of Jim Noonan-Jim allowed me to try it. It was a complicated case that I won at trial in Reno and argued on appeal. The Nevada Supreme Court affirmed. This next one was a trial and appeal in Hawaii. This one, the US Supreme Court citation, was a regulatory taking case for properties in the Tahoe area. In this next case the California Supreme Court affirmed my victory at trial where I was able to use my accounting background to establish a method of determining business good-will in eminent domain. I guess I don't have to explain the other cases you see here."

Browning had enough. He said:

"OK, I'll spend some time talking to Ted about his background. I'll talk to Joyce too. We'll get your website up and going. I'm sure you'll like it."

The firm got its website. The investment was enough to encourage John to learn how to use the internet.

CHAPTER ELEVEN

They had 1991 season tickets to watch the California Golden Bears play football in Memorial Stadium. Cal fans were undeterred by the reports that Memorial Stadium sat directly over the Hayward Fault. Two years earlier, on October 17, 1989 the Bay area suffered the *Loma Prieta earthquake*. The third game of the World Series was about to start. The local media referred to it as *The Bay Bridge Series*, as it was between the San Francisco Giants and the Oakland Athletics. At 5:04PM an earthquake rolled through the bay area with a magnitude of 7.1 on the Richter scale. Despite that disaster, including collapse of a portion of the Cypress Street Viaduct and of a small section of the Bay Bridge, Memorial Stadium was usually filled with fans loyal to the Bears.

It was unusually warm that day, with a mild off shore wind. Just before halftime, the Cal rooters saw a column of smoke off to the south. The smoke didn't last long; apparently, its source had been squelched.

The next morning John went downstairs to put on the coffee. *Is it foggy?* He asked himself. *Strange, it wasn't foggy yesterday.* He walked out through the dining room doors to the rear garden. *What a strange overcast! It smells like smoke. Is there a fire nearby? He* turned on the radio to hear about a fire in the Oakland hills in the area around the Caldecott tunnel. He hoped it wasn't near his parents' house on Fairlane Avenue. He went upstairs to listen to the radio with Sarah.

"People in the Hiller Highlands and the surrounding area have been ordered to vacate" the radio told them.

"My God," Sarah said, "that must be the same fire we saw yesterday at the game."

John phoned his mother.

"Oh, it won't come here", she said. "It's on the other side of the freeway."

"Maybe you'd better come to our house just to be safe."

"Oh no, I'll be all right. Dad has gone downtown for something. I'll be Ok here."

By 10 that morning, the radio reported that the fire had jumped the freeway. John phoned his mother.

"Yes, they tell us to get out. I guess I have to do it, but I don't think it will get this far."

"Mom, get in your car and come here right away."

"But what about Dad?"

"Mom, I heard on the radio they're not letting anyone in. People are ordered to get out. You get here and he'll be all right. He'll have to come here."

John's mother got to his house. Then, they waited to hear about his father.

"Do you think he tried to come home and got through?"

"No, Mom. Don't worry. They're not letting anyone in."

John said that to her. He didn't want to show that he was worried that Dad had gotten through, that he tried to get his computer and some files, and that perhaps he was trapped. *Maybe I should pray*. By noon, his Dad was at John's door. *Thank God*.

The family stayed by the TV into the night. All the homes on Fairlane Avenue were destroyed. The main worry reported by the media was that the fire would reach the Claremont Hotel. If that burned, the entire City of Berkeley would be next. On the other side, the fire had broached Piedmont. Without saying so, John was making plans to take the four of them to Tahoe. But by night, the fire was controlled. Its path into Piedmont was blocked by the Mountain View Cemetery. *The dead saved our home*.

The next day John went into the rear garden. The lawn, shrubs, flowers, trees and Eva were all covered by soot. Large cinders lay on the lawn and over Eva's face. No longer did she appear to be waiting for her lover's kiss.

John's parents stayed with them for ten days. By then their insurance paid for their stay at a hotel. Eventually they bought a home in San Leandro.

The Oakland Hills Fire destroyed 3,800 homes and killed 25 people. It covered 1,520 acres. Like the 1906 earthquake and fire in San Francisco, it was an urban tragedy.

CHAPTER TWELVE

In October, 1993, Ray Hayden retired from his accounting office. He remained a Certified Public Accountant, but limited his practice to a few of his closest clients.

Ray and Patricia had been in their new house in San Leandro ever since the Oakland Hills fire destroyed their home. Ray was in good health, except for the arthritis in his right knee. He had the replacement in January. By February Ray was ready for the prescribed physical therapy. He could do the exercises at the health club a short distance down the hill from his home. Because of his new knee he had to drive there.

When John and Sarah opened their door after returning home from Tahoe their phone was ringing. It was John's mother:

"Someone tried to kill Dad. They hit his head with something heavy as he was coming out of his car. They took his wallet. A man coming out of the club found him lying by his car with the car door open and blood all around. The ambulance took him to the hospital. Come quick."

John saw his father strapped to his hospital bed, in a coma but moaning and struggling as if to reach for something. His head was covered with blood-stained bandages as his gurney was rolled into surgery. He lingered for days. Sometimes, as when he'd try to tell a joke, he seemed to be on the road to recovery. Other times, he seemed near death. A month later, Ray's death came.

Corpus Christi Church was filled with the many friends and admirers who came to Ray's funeral. John described some of his father's history: That he was not among the privileged to go to college; that, during the depression he was a truck driver; and that after Pearl Harbor he enrolled into the Maritime Academy in order to serve in the Merchant Marine transporting troops and supplies across the Pacific. John told how his father studied accounting all during the war and how he became a Certified Public Accountant. Next to speak were Gregory and Jeffrey. As they spoke, John sat with his thoughts. *These guys have good looks, good brains, good jobs, they speak well, and I guess they're like their grandfather. But Sarah -she's the one who gets the credit for how well these guys turned out.*

Patricia remained in a state of shock, but she insisted on staying in her house in San Leandro. A few days after the funeral John went to check on his mother. She took him into the garage to point out the many things Ray had been storing there. By the inside of the garage door John saw a baseball bat standing against the wall. His first thought was of pleasant memories. His Dad loved baseball. In the 1930s, he played for a semi-pro team. John remembered how, when he was a kid, his Dad would take him to games at the Oaks' ballpark in Emeryville. He remembered how his Dad taught him to catch and hit. But, now, why is there a baseball bat in his garage? He hadn't played for years. Everything he had from the past was lost in the fire. Now, John's face turned pale.

"Mom, where did this bat come from?"

"I don't know. It was in his car. I took it out when I was looking for his things."

John remembered those words: *"They hit his head with something heavy as he was coming out of his car."*

John told his mother that since she was all right he was going home. On his way, he went to the San Leandro Police Station-with the bat.

At home in the early evening, John wondered about Eva. *Was she really at the Panama thing? She's stamped 'Frilli' and 'Firenzi.' If someone named Frilli carved her, certainly he's long gone. The Connollys said someone named Keeley bought her in 1915. He must be dead now. Dr. Connolly and now Ray Hayden- How many others has she seen come and go? How many wars has she been through? World War One, World War Two, Korea, Vietnam? She's still lying there, as if she's waiting for something.*

Ray Hayden's murder was never solved.

CHAPTER THIRTEEN

For the next few years John's law practice did well. With Ted working John could concentrate on the jury trials. And, he and Sarah could spend more leisure time at Tahoe.

March 5, 1998 was a routine Saturday morning. While Sarah slept, John sat at his desk. He often thought about his travels with the Navy around the Mediterranean. He had hoped to see those places again with Sarah.

Now, at 9:12, he answered the phone:

"Is this the John Hayden who was in the Sixth Fleet Band?" the voice asked.

"Yes. Who's this?" John answered.

"This is Bob Hunt, John."

Hunt played clarinet and alto sax in the band.

Hunt said: "We're planning a reunion in Washington D.C. in two weeks. I thought you might be a lawyer, and I found your website online. We hope you can make it."

"Gee, Bob, that's so soon, I don't know."

"John, Gene Martinelli, Cruz Santos and Bob Jorgensen will be there."

Gene, Cruz and Bob were John's best friends in the band.

John thought that he had only one trial set at that time. It was for a public agency, so he didn't have to worry about disappointing an owner. His opponent was an old friend who would agree to a continuance. He could leave Ted in charge of the office.

"I'll be there," he said.

"And John," Hunt said, "did you know that they've made the Salem a museum in Quincy, by Boston? It has a website. Take a look at it. See you in a couple of weeks."

John went upstairs to tell Sarah they were going to Washington. Then back to his computer he found the Salem website. He clicked on the announcement that a group of former Salem sailors were going to Europe on a tour starting from Boston on April 2. It would be a round-trip flight from Boston to Paris and six weeks in Europe, with travel by Eurail and lodging in three star hotels.

John phoned the number listed for the tour director-Joe Dunlevy, Boatswain's Mate 2nd on the Salem's 1957 crew. Joe answered. He said he was a travel agent now, that he was active in the Salem Association and that he had conducted a tour to Europe for the association last year. This one, he said, would be better yet.

"I was in the flag band from 1955 to1958," John told him.

"Yeah John", Joe answered, "I remember your band. It just so happens that we have an opening for one couple who just cancelled."

"So you're even including Villefranche?"

"Oh yeah-we're staying at the Welcome Hotel. It's been remodeled since we were there."

"As long as you don't tell the wives about the 0-2 level" John jibed.

Above a ship's weather deck the levels of the superstructure are labeled 0-1, 0-2 and up. Villefranche Sur Mer is part of the *Alpes Maritime*, where rocky hills ascend abruptly from the Mediterranean. The Welcome Hotel, Mom Germaine's and other restaurants are on the *Fleet Landing*, or shore level. Narrow stairways lead up to the higher levels. What the sailors called *the 0-2 level* was home to bars and prostitutes. Joe told John that *Queenie's* was the only bar remaining up there, Queenie was in her 80s and no longer employed young ladies. But, he said, the place was filled with photos and memorabilia of the Sixth Fleet days.

"We're planning a dinner party at Queenie's; the wives will understand," Joe said.

"Count us in", John replied.

They had just a few days to prepare for their trip to the East Coast and Europe. For the reunion they'd fly from SFO to Dulles. After the reunion, they'd take the train to Boston. Then they'd fly from Logan to Paris with the group from the Salem. The flight home would be from Paris to Logan, with a connecting flight to bring John and Sarah back to SFO.

John thought there was no way he could prepare for the reunion. But for the trip to Europe, he had two things in mind: to review the French he had forgotten during the past 40 years and to research the origin of Eva. Eva showed only one thing about her history. On her smooth marble base was an embedded printing: *Frilli, Firenze.*

What about that 1915 Panama Pacific Exposition story? John asked himself, *isn't there some way to prove that?*

At the Oakland Public Library John found a section full of books and photos about the 1915 Exposition. His search revealed nothing about Eva and nothing about Frilli. He wondered whether by some miracle he could be more successful in Florence, if only he could get there.

The group was to spend 4 days in Rome and then board a train late in the afternoon for an overnight trip to Montreau, Switzerland. On line John discovered that the train from Rome to Montreau passed through Florence. *So why not go to Florence earlier in the day and join the group as their train passed through Florence that evening?* John phoned Dunleavy.

"Everyone will have a Eurail pass." Joe said. "It allows so many days. As long as you take the train from Rome to Florence and then get on the train to Montreau on the same day, you can do that."

John took pictures of Eva to carry to Florence. *Maybe there will be records or someone with information about Frilli.*

CHAPTER FOURTEEN

Bob Hunt reserved rooms at a hotel in Fairfax, Virginia. Through the Navy School of Music he got copies of the big band arrangements they played 40 years earlier.

The first night would be a jam session, with Gene Martinelli on tenor, Cruz Santos on trombone, Jack Foster on string bass and John on piano.

John called off the first tune: *All the things you are, A flat*. They played it as if they were still in the Hot Club in Nice. All the old stand-by tunes followed: *B flat Blues, I'll Remember April, Body and Soul, Indiana, Yesterdays, Over the Rainbow, Blue Monk, Georgia on my Mind, Lady Be Good*- on into the evening.

The next day the whole band rehearsed the dance band arrangements and some military marches for their concert for themselves and the wives. The reunion ended with the intention to do it sometime again.

John and Sarah boarded the train in DC to go to Boston. John wondered why he hadn't noticed the beauty of that old train station 40 plus years ago.

The group gathered at Logan Airport. It was Sarah's first flight across the pond. To John's surprise, she was worry-free.

They arrived at *Orly- L'aéroport*. With passports in hand they waited "*pour passer la police*". Next they had to "*passer le douanier*".

John had been reviewing his French. Here was his chance.

The douanier asked: "Vous n'avez rien à déclarer" ? John answered: " Rien."

Then the douanier asked: "Vous êtes tous les deux?" John responded: "Oui. C'est ma femme."

Looking disgusted, the douanier said: "Ça va. Passez. Vous pouvez passer. Allez-y, allez-y! Passez."

They boarded the *RER*-the inter-urban rail system that extends from Paris beyond the limits of the *Métro*, including Orly Airport. Dunlevy announced that they were to get off quickly at the stop for the *Gare d'Est*, as they were to stay across the street at *L'Hôtel Français*. John and Sarah went to their assigned room with its wall-to-wall bed and its closet-size bathroom.

John had been to Paris before. In 1955 his Navy Band was invited to participate in *L'Exposition Nautique*, put on by the French Government. *L'Expostion Nautique* was a display on the Seine of boats and ships from around the world. The band was to play, in uniform, for one hour on each of 5 days. In return, France gave the band a suite of rooms at a hotel and assigned a full-time guide to show the men around Paris, including Versailles and *Fontainebleau*. Nights were free to visit the jazz clubs on *Le Rive Gauche*. Then, the weather was superb.

Now the weather was muggy and there was no air-conditioning. John wondered: *Would all the hotels on this trip be like this?* But Sarah was delighted. She had no memories to cause her to be a disappointed.

From the next day on Paris was wonderful. John and Sarah did it all-*La Rive Gauche, Le Quartier Latin, Le Jardin du Luxembourg, L'île de la Cité, Notre Dame, L'île Saint-Louis, Les Champs-Elysées, l'Arc de Triomphe, La Place de la Concorde, Le Musée d'Órsay, La tour Eiffel, Montmartre, Sacré-Cœur, Le Louvre-* ---all by the Métro and *à pied*. Paris is loaded with art. John noticed that in 1955, but not so much as he did now. Yes, the paintings were wonderful. But now he especially noticed the sculpture virtually everywhere he looked. Most of the statues were in white marble, many by Italian artists.

They enjoyed *le déjeuner* at small neighborhood restaurants and bistros where John could practice his French. While the others maintained the American tradition of dinner at 6:00, Sarah and John had been on the European meal schedule for many years.

Sarah had always been an excellent cook. More, she was an artist about meal presentation. For most of their dinners Sarah set a table with burning candles and fresh flowers. So now, in France, *les diners* at 9 or 10 continued as their norm.

John's love for Sarah had never waned. But the years of raising children and making a living had made its expression routine. Now he looked into her deep brown eyes as he did when they first met. He held her warm and shapely body with the passion for which Paris was known.

On the late afternoon of the fifth day in Paris Dunlevy got everyone across the street to the *Gar d"Est* to board the train for their overnight ride to Munich for one day, and then on to Salzburg, Austria.

Usually a light sleeper, John slept surprisingly well that night on the train. He and Sarah awoke early to enjoy the breathtaking alpine scenery as the train traversed France, Switzerland and Austria. They arrived in Munich in the late morning. Dunlevy had arranged for a sightseeing bus and guide to show the group the Bavarian attractions. It was Ascension Thursday, a holiday in Munich. Most of the stores were closed. But, the beer gardens flourished. Of course, they gathered at the *Hofbrauhaus*.

Sarah thought they should at least visit a church. One close by, not the main cathedral, was upstairs and comfortably small. But its statues and paintings were of overwhelming beauty. The pews were filled with well-dressed parishioners. Mass started just as John and Sarah sat down. As the priest approached the altar it seemed as if everyone began singing in operatic-quality. Exiting with the crowd, many young Germans volunteered to welcome them in perfect English.

Late that afternoon they were on the train again. This time for the ninety minute ride to Salzburg. A bus was waiting there to take them to *Hotel Trumer*. It was delightful--so much better than their room in Paris.

They tasted all of Salzburg's attractions: *Mozart's birthplace, the Hohensalzburg fortress*, an evening concert in the main hall of the castle, a tour to the home of *Sound of Music* and a marionette show. As in France, they were able to enjoy the local cuisine in picturesque restaurants at their preferred late hour. And, as in Paris, John took special note of the statuary that seemed to be everywhere.

On their third morning in Salzburg, the group boarded the train for another overnight journey-- to Venice, Italy.

Dunlevy should have planned better on this one. Only one day in Venice! Of all places, Venice requires more time.

They arrived at the train station in the morning. They checked their baggage until their return that night. They walked over the *Rialto Bridge*, through the narrow alleyways, over more bridges and they arrived at *St. Mark's Square*.

John had been to Venice during his Sixth Fleet days. As he remembered it, the weather was always pleasant there. But today, on Sarah's first sight of St. Mark's Square, it was raining. Sarah seemed not to mind that at all. They saw all they could -the *glass blowers*, the *vaporettos*, the *gondolas*, the *Piazza San Marco* and its *Basilica*, and, of course, the *bridge of sighs*'. They finished the day at a restaurant recommended by a waiter at the Square. It was good. It was authentic. But somehow, they felt as if they had been set up. Going back to the train station John thought: *So many marble statues in Venice. Somehow, I didn't notice that 40 years ago.*

They joined the group for another overnighter-to Nice, France.

From 1955 to 1958 John's Navy Band was stationed aboard the flagship of the Sixth Fleet, whose *homeport* was Villefranche Sur Mer. There the ship anchored in the bay adjacent to Cap Ferrat. Only In Villefranche could John take long shore leaves and wear civilian clothes. In Nice, adjacent to Villefranche, John discovered a small restaurant and "pension" at 6 Rue DeLille. It was owned by Lucien and Mimi Guige. While their ship was at Villefranche John and his friends rented the upstairs rooms. While their ship was at sea they could store their civilian clothes in the closet in the utility room. Lucien kept a ledger of charges for the rooms and the meals they had at the restaurant.

Nice is within *La Cote d'Azur*. The English call the area *the French Riviera*. In French it is aptly named *Les Alpes Maritimes*. Now John was going back to Nice-this time with Sarah. They slept on the train from Venice. They awoke early enough to watch the Ligurian coast as they made their way north from Genova. Dunlevy had hired a bus and guide to bring the group from the train station in Nice to the *Welcome Hotel* in Villefranche. They passed the old port and ascended onto *le Moyenne Corniche*.

As they passed through Villefranche, the group again saw the commercial buildings, the ancient Citadel, the monument and the park. There the bus turned off the Corniche for the rapid descent down the cobblestone road to *Villefranche Sur Mer,* where it stopped at *Quai Amiral Courbet.* The travelers stepped onto *the fleet landing*, carrying their baggage into the *Welcome Hotel*.

John and Sarah were assigned a room on the third floor with a balcony overlooking the fleet landing. It was comfortable, fairly spacious and charming. From the balcony they could see the flagstone pier, *le chapel de Saint Pierre*, designed by *Jacques Cousteau*, the fisherman and their boats, the clear blue water of the bay, the beach, the train station and *Cap Ferrat*.

At the shoreline were the buildings and the narrow cobble-stoned roadway. The beach formed a half-circle ending at the tip of *Cap Ferrat*. The girls still wore bikinis, but now only the bottoms. John noticed a big change: Now they shaved under their arms! He wondered where that trend would lead. He thought: *Topless is nice, but they're lucky Dr.Connolly isn't here on St. Patrick's Day with his green paint!* But as the girls lay prone their breasts sagged. John thought: *Not like Eva. I'm back to Villefranche after forty years, seeing girls all but nude and I'm thinking of Eva!*

Next to the *Welcome Hotel* were a row of restaurants, small boutiques and other small hotels. The first restaurant was still as John remembered it: *La Mere Germaine*. "Mom Germaine" started her restaurant in 1938. As Villefranche Sur Mer became its homeport she became known as *the mother of the Sixth fleet*. For their first dinner at *La Mere Germaine* John and Sarah were greeted by Mom Germaine's grandson. As he escorted them to their table John told him:

"J'étais ici il y a quarante ans, avec le sixième flotte. Je me souviens bien de votre grand-mère."

He shouted to his father on the other side of the restaurant:

"Papa, c'était matelot américain. Il se souvient de grand-maman."

The wine was on the house.

The following day John and Sarah enjoyed their *petit déjeuner* on their balcony as they watched the fishermen returning with their catch. Today they would explore Nice. Together they left the hotel and walked up the steep cobble-stoned road to get the bus. Sarah wore a white dress and high-heeled shoes, as if she were there in the days of F. Scott Fitzgerald. They rested at the park and watched a group of elderly men as they played *le ball*. John was aiming his camera when a young spectator warned:

"Ce n'est pas sage, monsieur. On ne veut pas de photo."

Remembering how seriously these men took this game, John put his camera back in its case as he and Sarah boarded the bus.

The bus station in Nice was as John remembered it. But as he and Sarah walked up *L'Avenue St. Jean Baptiste* towards *Rue DeLille* he was overwhelmed by the change. To their right the wide creek had been filled in and was now covered by *Le Théatre, Le Musée* and *L'Acropolis*. The Acropolis included the International Congress Centre and the Exhibition Centre. It covered 17,000 square meters of what John remembered to be an empty creek bed. To the left of the *Musée* they entered *Rue DeLille*- now a busy one-way thoroughfare adjacent to what had become an important center of Nice.

They came to number 6. It was a new and different building. Instead of a restaurant the ground floor contained a store selling window coverings. John asked the young man behind the counter:

« Excusez-moi, monsieur. Est-ce que vous connaissez monsieur Lucien Giuge ? »

« Non, monsieur, je ne le connais pas. »

« Il y avait ici un restaurant qui s'appelle le Restaurant Delille. Savez-vous où ce restaurant se trouve maintenant? »

« Non, monsieur. Je n'ai pas entendu dire de ce restaurant-là. »

He tried not to show his disappointment to Sarah. But she knew, as she always did.

"Let's go into this little restaurant at the end of the street", she said. "There must be someone there who remembers."

Reluctantly, John went in. He asked the lady *à la caisse* the same questions and got the same answers. His head was low when a young waitress approached. « Monsieur. Je connais Madame Guige. Elle habit un appartement là-bas, à 6 Rue Delille. Sonnez à sa porte. Je crois qu'elle reste chez-elle aujourd'hui. »

Above the window store at 6 Rue DeLille was a second story. A doorway with mailboxes and doorbells was at ground level. John looked and saw her name: "Madame Lucien Guige." John rang.

« Oui »

« Madame Guige, c'est John Hayden. Je visitais chez-vous il y a quarante ans, quand j'étais matelot American. »

« Ah, oui, Monsieur. Entrez. »

Their visit with this sweet old lady made their day. Mimi told them of Lucien's death a few years earlier. Lucien had sold the building, reserving a life-estate in one apartment for her. Mimi treated Sarah as if she had known her all her life. Language was no barrier. Mimi showed her all the family photos. Of course much of the conversation was about Mimi's cat. The French love their pets. John took Mimi's picture as she stood arm in arm with Sarah. As they left, Mimi said:

« Je vous embrasse. Bon voyage, et merci bien. Enchantée de vous voir encore. »

They walked down to the *Promenade des Anglais*. Now the French girls were dressed in jeans and tank tops. Looking at Sarah, though, he was reminded of the female beauty he thought would always be a part of *La Cote d"Azur*. They entered the *Negresco*. They ordered lunch and acted like the tourists they were, paying accordingly.

Their tour of the City followed- *à pied*." They walked to *Le Cour Saleya, Le Vieux* Nice, *Le Musée Matisse, La Cathédrale Saint-Nicolas, Le Jardin Albert 1er, Le Vieux Port* and back to the bus station to return to Villefranche. Strange it was that John didn't remember noticing that Nice had so many marble statues when he was there in the Navy.

Back to the *Welcome Hotel* John fell exhausted on the bed. It was dark when John awoke. Sarah had chosen their restaurant for the evening-*La Fille du Pecheur*. The fresh fish was marvelous.

The next night they ate at the next restaurant in line. On a stair as if overlooking the tables sat a little white dog-some kind of terrier. The owner told Sarah the little dog's name was *Stanley*.

Sarah has a habit unforgivable by the French-she puts ice in her red wine! Somehow, they make an exception for her. The waiter had put a bowl of ice at her side. Sarah called Stanley. He was happy to run up and jump onto her lap. Stanley gave her one quick kiss and then proceeded to lick all the water out of the ice bowl. John and Sarah laughed. They, like the French, love their pets.

Chapter Fifteen

Four days later the group was off again, this time for the short train ride down the coast to the *Cinque Terre Villages*. At the train station it was a short wait for the one marked *Ventimiglia*-the first stop in Italy. From there they proceeded down the Ligurian coast for their stop at *Santa Margherita*. A bus was waiting to take them to the *Lauren Hotel*.

The Lauren's rooms overlooked the sea. Each had a patio-balcony under awnings that rolled out with the push of a button. In the park was a statue of *Christopher Columbus, Santa Margherita*'s most famous son.

John and Sarah boarded the bus that runs over to Portofino. They traversed the narrow and winding road attached to the steep slopes descending to the sea.

Portofino was breathtaking, especially the yachts and their bikini-clad crews. John and Sarah selected a *ristorante* for their *pranzo*. Of course they had it served *all'aperto*.

The beauty of the Ligurian coast was only diminished by John's anticipation of his visit to Florence, where he hoped to discover more about Eva. After three days at the Lauren Hotel the group boarded the train for their next stop: Rome.

The *Columbo Hotel* was small and quaint. John and Sarah's room was charming. In its center was a circular ladder-like staircase leading to the bathroom on the floor above. It was over the rear courtyard. At night they heard the laughter from the parties going on somewhere down there. Later in the night they were visited by cats who were apparently accustomed to enter through open hotel windows. *Colazione* was served on the hotel's roof, where much of the beauty of the City could be viewed.

In their three days in Rome they saw the *Fountain of Trevi,* the *Vatican,* the *Coliseum*, the *Spanish Steps*, the *Pantheon-* and they delighted in the cuisine of the many restaurants along the way. They attended Mass said by Pope John Paul at St. Peter's Square. They planned to visit the Sistine Chapel after Mass, but the line was impossible. "Domani, è Lunedi"-come back tomorrow an elderly gentleman told them. "Good idea," John told Sarah, "but we're getting on the train to Florence tomorrow. We'd better get here early."

Chapter Sixteen

That Monday morning they got to the Vatican at 10. The line outside the Sistine Chapel was just as long as it had been Sunday. And, they discovered that they had to circle around, seemingly endlessly, to gain entrance. Inside the Chapel was dark and crowded. What hell Michelangelo must have endured! Having seen it, they were free to hail a taxi to get to the train station for their trip to Florence.

Bob Dunlevy had promised to take their suitcases onto his later train from Rome to Montreau. So all John and Sarah had to do was to board the same train at 8:30 PM as it passed through Florence. But because of their long wait at the Sistine Chapel they didn't get to Florence until 4:15. John was upset. *Now, how will we have time to find out anything about Eva?* But Sarah said they'd find something. She went into the first hotel she saw. She asked where they might find sculptures. The clerk told her to cross the bridge over the Arno River and walk along a street named Via Dei Fossi, where they'd find some sculpture studios.

Arriving there they saw a studio loaded with marble statuary. The owner, in a wheelchair, spoke English.

"Pardon me, Sir. I have a statue that says "Frilli, Firenze. Would you know anything about that?"

"Frilli? Why that's right next door. Look there-you see it?"

John's heart pounded. How lucky could they be!

They entered the Frilli Gallery. A lady approached.

"Hello, my name is Gloria. May I help you?"

"Yes, thank you. We have an old statue in our yard."

"Oh. Where is your home?"

"We live in the San Francisco area. Our town is Piedmont."

"Oh, I know that. I spent some time in Berkeley. Tell me about your statue."

"I brought these pictures. She's life-sized, lying nude in a hammock. You see here, she needs a good cleaning. I was told she was purchased at the 1915 Panama Pacific Exhibition in San Francisco. Do you have records here that might show that?"

"No. What we have here doesn't go back that far. She is beautiful, though. I've never seen any statue quite like that."

"Well, what about that inscription? It's on the base of the statue. See here, it's stamped 'Frilli, Firenze.' "

"Yes. That shows she's from here."

"Does it mean that the sculptor was Frilli himself?"

"Not necessarily. He had many students. Many statues would be duplicated a few times, not always by the same person. I can tell you that your statue is Carrara marble. At that time all Frilli statues were. Most of what you see here today is also Carrara marble."

"I was also hoping that you could tell me how I should try to clean her. I don't dare to use a high-pressure hose. Is there some kind of cleaner I should know about?"

"I'd advise you to do nothing unless you contact someone who is an expert with Carrara marble."

"Well, please keep these pictures. If you ever find any more information, here's my card. Please write or phone-reverse the charge. I really want to find more about her."

"I'll let you know if I find anything about your statue. Please enjoy the rest of your trip."

John and Sarah left the Frilli Gallery delighted that it still existed, but disappointed with how little they discovered about Eva. Even a trip to Florence couldn't verify the Connolly story about her being at the1915 Exhibition.

Their dinner *al aperto* at a *ristorante* by the *Piazza di Santa Maria Novella* was early for them, much too early for Italians, but they had to make the sacrifice to be waiting when the train passed through the station.

They made it! Dunlevy was waiting. Their bags were in their compartment. It was supposed to be first class. It was second, but why complain? They slept just as well. The next morning they arrived in Montreau, Switzerland. A guide and bus waited there to escort the group to the 1000 year old *Chateau of Chillon*. It was beautiful, as was the blue lake it adorned. The bus took them back to board the *Crystal Panoramic Express* to Lenk. John took a close-up photo of Sarah, as she smiled in the dining car. Anyone can take pictures of mountains! After a picnic in Lenk the group boarded the train for their 2 day stay at *Interlaken; Hotel Carlton.*

Yes, Interlaken was beautiful too. The train took them back to Paris, again for 3 days at the *Hotel Francais*. Then the *RER* took them back to *Orley,* American Airlines took them to Boston and SFO. Waiting for them by the baggage claim was Gregory. His Volvo station wagon took the travelers home. John got a good night's sleep while thinking *who knows? Maybe Gloria might discover something about Eva*.

Chapter Seventeen

A letter dated January 7, 2000 came from Florence. The envelope said "Frilli Gallery". It was from Gloria. *Imagine that! After all this time! Maybe she had new information about Eva going to the Panama Pacific Exposition*. John opened the letter:

Dear Mr. and Mrs. Hayden:

The enclosed note may interest you. Your statue must be worth more than I thought. This one was sold by Sotheby's for $575,000. Sincerely, Gloria. Enclosed was a page from Sotheby's with a picture of a statue like Eva. This one was pristine. The white patina was smooth and untarnished. The page gave the address and phone number of the antique dealer who had participated in the sale. John placed the call.

"I saw the announcement about the Frilli statue you sold. We have one like that at our home in Piedmont. I was hoping you could tell me something about its history. Also, it needs cleaning. Can you tell me how to do it?"

"I'd have to see it. I'll be in your area next month. I could come by to see your statue."

"It's in our back yard."

"I see your phone number. I'll call to let you know when it will be. In the meanwhile, don't try to clean it. That takes an expert."

On March 1 John got the call. Eva would be examined the next day at 2:30. On time, the doorbell rang:

"Hello. I'm Mario. Here's my card."

"Hello Mario. Thanks for coming all this way. Come right through these doors to the patio. There she is beyond the lawn, next to the wall."

Mario took his time in examining Eva, taking photos as he progressed.

"There aren't many of these left." He told John. "I heard of one in a cemetery in Brazil. Statues like this were often used to decorate gravesites."

John thought he should ask: "What do you think she's worth as she is here now?"

Mario took his time to answer: "You'd have to sell her to a dealer-someone who could have her restored. That may bring sixty to seventy thousand dollars."

Trying not to show his surprise John thought: *Maybe selling Eva could make up for the money I've been shelling out for Tahoe.* He asked: "Would she be worth that to you?"

Hesitating, Mario went closer to Eva. "That broken piece will have to be replaced. There are very few craftsmen I'd allow to touch her. It would be quite an investment to make her saleable. I couldn't offer more than that in her condition now."

Thinking he should change the subject John said: "Well, we didn't intend to sell her. We hoped to find out about her history. The story we got was that she was bought at the 1915 Panama Exhibition in San Francisco."

"I don't know about that", Mario answered. "She apparently came from the Frilli Gallery. Whatever you do, don't try to clean her yourself."

John looked at Sarah. She seemed upset. *Why? We got something free we can sell for $70,000,* John thought. Sarah apparently didn't share his enthusiasm.

"I have to leave", Mario said. "Think it over."

The next day John got Sarah's reluctant OK to counter-offer $90,000. In the mail a week later the offer was accepted, along with a written contract that John signed and returned. Mario came with a moving van as John took the cashier's check to the bank. John watched as Eva was loaded into the van. Climbing the stairs to their bedroom he heard Sarah crying. On the bed, face down, Sarah said: "I should have stopped them. I should have said no. I feel terrible about this. I feel that we're going to be punished for this. Bad things will happen-I know—I know."

CHAPTER EIGHTEEN

2001 was a difficult year for John. The arthritis in his hands made his piano playing painful. The Piedmont home was showing signs of deferred maintenance. The Tahoe home was no longer a novelty. The boys and their families didn't go there and for John it was just another place to bring his worries.

During that year a series of events caused the collapse of John's law practice. In January his secretary told him she had to quit. Her husband was being discharged and they would return to their home in Georgia. In February Ted announced that he was moving his family out of Oakland, that he was joining another law firm, and that the clients he had been serving wanted to stay with him. In March, John received notice that when his office lease expired at the end of the month his rent would triple. The former owner of the building, his friend and client, had sold it to a national real estate company.

John blamed himself for the loss of his clients. After he hired Ted he began spending more time at Tahoe. To avoid traffic, he and Sarah would leave Friday morning and return the following Monday. It became typical for him to attend to his practice only three days a week. So it was Ted who served the clients. No wonder they wanted to stay with him.

Now John's practice was gone. He thought: *This wouldn't be happening if it weren't for that house. But we can't sell it now.*

Sarah still cries about selling Eva. He wanted some excuse to forget his troubles. He told himself, *after all these years I deserve a sabbatical. Maybe after a year something will happen. Maybe I'll get an offer from a law firm-maybe I'll get a chance to teach in a law school-something!*

Chapter Nineteen

It was January 15, 2002. Two weeks ago the speech therapist in Reno had recommended that John read aloud. Maybe that was routine for stroke victims. Now, back home in Piedmont, he mustered up his nerve. He thought, *why not the Bible*?

Starting at Genesis, he read aloud: *"And God said, Let the earth bring forth the living creatures in its kind, cattle and creeping things"*. John thought about how those creeping things caused his stroke at Tahoe on New Year's Eve day.

Soon after John and Sarah bought the Tahoe house they began to be challenged by the "creeping things." First were the carpenter ants. Then, on summer nights bats would hover over the front porch leaving droppings for John to clean in the morning. Then the woodpeckers-the sound of their pecking on the side of the house was like gunfire. Then there were mice. John saw a deer mouse in the basement. Fred Butler, who lived across the street, showed John an article reporting that deadly "Hanta-Virus" could be contracted from exposure to feces of deer mice. One case had occurred nearby. The victim had suffered a loss of speech followed by an agonizing death.

But the biggest battle was with squirrels. The recreation room downstairs had to accommodate a large rock. Houses built around and over rocks are typical at Tahoe. Part of the rock was outside the house; part jutted into the room. There John saw it- a squirrel perched on top of the rock. Now he had to do something. He covered the space between the rock and the wall with steel wool.

The day after Christmas in 2001 John and Sarah drove from Piedmont to Tahoe. Gregory, Michelle and their two girls had already arrived. The next morning John heard a squirrel scratching inside the wall upstairs.

While Gregory was loading his car to go home, the girls decided to make animal feeders. Sarah helped them spread peanut butter and birdseed over pinecones. After they put the feeders around the yard they said goodbye. John put the birdseed back in the basement. Then he saw that the top of the plastic container was riddled with holes. A bewildering thought turned into fear: *Could it be that the deer mice got into the birdseed? Could it be that their feces are in the seeds? Could the kids have been exposed to Hanta-Virus? Could I be exposed now? Should I tell Sarah? No, she'd only worry.*

On New Year's Eve day the scratching noise came back. It seemed to come from the top of the shower. Looking into the shower John saw a squirrel's nose pushing its way through the wallpaper. He banged his fist on the wall. The squirrel retreated. Then, not a sound! John decided to cover that hole with steel wool. That would give him time to take his morning shower and think about his next move.

Shaved and dressed, he sat down with Sarah to discuss the plan of the day. His every word came out garbled. What was happening? His thoughts were intact. He felt normal. But he couldn't talk. *Is it the Hanta-Virus?*

Sarah telephoned Fred Butler. She whispered: "Something's wrong with John. I think he's had a stroke."

John agreed to let Sarah drive him to Barton Hospital in South Lake Tahoe. Before getting into the car, he went to his desk and wrote a note:

"Test me for Hanta-Virus. If confirmed, tell my wife. Our grandchildren may be in danger." He hid the note from Sarah.

They ushered him into ER while Sarah took care of his admission. The nurse said: "Strip, put on this gown and lie on that gurney". This was his chance, he thought, as he handed her the secret note. She took it away and closed the curtain behind her. John waited on the gurney. The curtain finally opened as the nurse reappeared.

"OK, Mr. Hayden, what seems to be the trouble with you and this-what is it-'Hanta-Virus'? That's a new one on me."

He tried to tell her about the deer mice, but his words made no sense.

"Mice? What mice? Did they bite you?" she asked.

No, he thought, he had to make her understand. He tried to explain. His words made no sense.

"OK, calm down, Mr. Hayden. The mice can't hurt you now" the nurse said as she closed the curtain again."

After another long wait she came back.

"OK, Mr. Hayden, the doctor told me to hook you up on this I.V. Make a fist. Now, did anything else happen to you this morning?"

He tried again: "Th- squi-rr-le."

"The squirrel, Mr. Hayden? I thought it was a mouse! And what did the squirrel do to you?" Not waiting for an answer she again closed the curtain.

"He's delirious", he heard her telling the doctor.

Again she came back. "The doctor has given you something to calm you down. We'll put it into your I.V. You'll be feeling fine in just a few minutes."

The "something" was beginning to take effect. John was aware of being put into some kind of tunnel before he had another long wait behind the curtain.

This time it was the doctor who came in.

"OK, Mr. Hayden, the cat-scan shows you had a stroke, with bleeding in your left-frontal lobe. That explains your loss of speech. I've ordered a helicopter to take you to Washoe Med in Reno. They're equipped to deal with your situation. Please relax until it comes. It shouldn't be long."

The curtain closed. John thought: *A stroke! It wasn't the mice!*

Sarah held his hand while the crew wheeled the gurney towards the helicopter. She bent over and kissed him. "Everything will be OK", she whispered. They loaded him aboard and he was on his way to Reno.

As the doctor walked Sarah to her car he asked:

"What kind of medications was he taking?"

"All for his arthritis."

"How long has he had that?"

"Well, let's see, it was soon after he sold Eva-so that's about two years now. It drives him crazy- he plays the piano. So he takes aspirin and those other painkillers. Every time I say something about it he says they don't hurt him."

"Does he take anything else?"

"He does take that stuff, Gingko, or whatever it's called. He says it helps his circulation."

"Mrs. Hayden, your husband had an inter-cranial hemorrhage. Those things are blood-thinners. I can't say they caused his stroke, but they sure didn't help."

The doctor waited as Sarah got into her car. "Are you all right?" he asked.

"I'm fine. Will I have time to drive to Reno before they have to do anything serious to him?"

"You'll have time. It will take some time for his sedative to wear off. Just be careful driving, especially tonight."

In Reno they loaded John onto the gurney and wheeled him through a maze of hallways. With the sedative he had no idea of how much time passed. He was vaguely aware of being pushed again into a tunnel. A voice came from outside.

"Mr. Hayden, you have to hold perfectly still in there".

Then came the shots. *"Click, click, click-bang, bang, bang''*– After what seemed to be hours listening to gunfire he finally came out of the tunnel.

"OK, Mr. Hayden, that's it. Thanks for holding still."

The MRI convinced the doctors that John wouldn't need surgery. Then there were two days of sessions with the speech therapist. She called it *aphasia*. She asked:

"Do you sing?"

"Ah littow bid", he answered.

"Well, try singing. Singing uses different brain cells. It often happens that people can sing words they couldn't say by speaking. And, above all, speak slowly for a while."

She told him he might experience depression- that many people recovering from stroke do. But *oh no*, he told himself, *not me. It's because of these damn things that have been happening to me. I lost my law practice, I lost my office, I got this damn arthritis and now I've lost my speech. All because of that damn house.*

CHAPTER TWENTY

In June, 2003 John renewed his appointments with Dr. Kern, the specialist who diagnosed his arthritis a few years ago.

John refused to take Aleve, or drugs like it, telling Kern that they caused his stroke. Kern administered a cortisone shot in John's left thumb and told him to come back in one month.

A month later John was back, complaining that the shot was worthless. This time Kern sent him to a therapist to be fitted for a thumb splint. Back again two months later, John said that didn't help at all. He felt the pain while he played the piano. That was no place for a thumb splint.

Kern told him:

"You know, John, I have golfer patients who have the same thing. They just play through it."

"I'm not talking about golf," John grumbled, "The piano isn't just my hobby."

"Well, John, let's go over this again. When does the pain in your thumbs hurt the most?"

"As I said-when I play the piano."

"How about when you do other things, like opening jars or doing garden work?"

"Very little."

"So you spend a lot of time playing the piano, and that's when it hurts the most?"

"No. I don't have much time for that anymore-and no one cares."

"Tell me again how the pain starts."

"It's in what you doctors call the first metacarpal-the joint that connects the thumb to the wrist. You don't think I remembered you told me that, do you? I even went on line to check it out. It's also a little bit in this top joint on my left finger-the index finger, but not as much."

"Well, we've tried everything. The cortisone shot fixes it for most people. Not for you. We tried the thumb splint. Now you tell me that didn't help. You say you don't have much of a problem except when you play the piano. And, you say you don't play much anymore. So I wonder if this thing has become magnified in your mind."

"So, what's next? Less piano playing and more booze?"

"John, I'm going to recommend that you see Doctor Freidman. He's a Psychiatrist. His office is in Oakland, close to you. Here's his card. Maybe you should talk to him and see why this thing seems to be bothering you so much."

On his drive home, John fumed: *I don't need a shrink. So Kern thinks it's in my head! It's arthritis, damn it. Maybe Sarah would be better off if I gave up the piano. There must be some kind of operation. Then we'll sell that damn house.*

CHAPTER TWENTY ONE

John finally admitted to himself that he should give Dr. Kern's advice a try. *I'll see what the shrink has to say about my arthritis. He'll see it's not in my head and send me back to Kern. Then, maybe I might get some relief.*

The appointment was made: Friday, October 15, 2004. Approaching the converted Victorian house used for Freidman's office John thought, *the shrink wants his office to look like a house. I'll tolerate this today only.*

The first discussion was with Freidman's secretary. John agreed to pay fees for each visit upon arrival. It was to be by check-Sarah was not to know about this.

Into Freidman's private office John was comfortably seated. He felt relieved that he didn't have to lie on a couch. Freidman sat to the side with his pencil and notebook. John admitted to himself that with his beard and tattered tweed jacket with patches on the sleeves this guy looked rather avuncular. The questions followed: What were his likes as a child, his relationship with his parents, whether he got along with his teachers, his first sexual experience--the same script John expected. Then:

"On your medical history I see you had a stroke", Friedman said. "And I hear that you stumble on some of your words-that's called aphasia. I assume that there's no like effect on your thinking or writing, right?"

"That's right."

"Well, don't worry about your words. Please continue to speak slowly. These notes I'm taking will look like you've spoken each word without a flaw."

Friedman spent some time writing something in his notes before he continued:

"We all have some kind of health problems. Tell me about yours- Any health issues today, aside from your stroke?"

"No. "

Friedman changed the subject. He asked: "Are your parents still alive?"

"They're both gone. My father was murdered."

"Can you tell me about that?"

"Because of the Oakland Hills Fire they moved to San Leandro. He was killed there."

"Do you blame his death on that fire?"

'It wouldn't have happened without it."

John thought: *But we got over the fire and even Dad's death. We could still be happy until I sold Eva. I won't tell this guy about that.*

"Siblings?"

"One brother-fifteen years younger."

"Did you get along with him?"

"Yes, but because of the age difference it was unusual. For most of his early years I was away in the Navy. When I came back he was more like my child."

"And your wife-what's her name?"

"Sarah."

"You're happily married?"

"We were."

"And you have children?"

"Yes. Two sons. They're adults now, with families of their own."

"The first born-what's his name?"

"Gregory. He's in real estate-He's a well- known appraiser-Good at his job and a great husband and father."

"And the other son?"

"That's Jeffrey. He's in the process of leaving a successful career in computers to pursue the interest he's had for a long time-in religion. He's an assistant pastor and on his way to an advanced degree in theology."

"It sounds as if you've done a good job in raising your sons."

"Not me. Sarah gets the credit for that."

"So you have grand kids?"

"Greg and Jeff each have two daughters-quite beautiful-they get that from Sarah."

"Are you retired?"

"Involuntarily. I hate it."

"In your early years, did you have some special abilities?"

"Well, my mother always wanted me to be in show business. At age four I took tap dancing lessons. I even danced at the 1940 World's Fair on Treasure Island. Then, all the kids-including my cousins, had to perform and sing. I did a lot of that. Later on my sport was swimming. My coach was Al Kolunki. I swam in a lot of meets-I won some. Then came the piano. After high school I played piano bar in a resort-I was the 'master of ceremonies.' In the Navy I was the spokesman for the band."

"Do you miss doing things like that today?"

"I'll admit to that. Yes, I am an extrovert-you can put that in your notes."

"Tell me about your education."

"Public school for the first eight years. A Catholic high school-I must admit it was a good education. After the Navy I went through Cal as an undergraduate, thanks to the GI Bill. Then, three years of Law School, thanks to Sarah's working to put me through."

"So you were a lawyer. Did you like doing that?"

"It was my profession. I was a trial lawyer. Music was only my hobby-I play piano."

"Did you have a specialty as a lawyer?"

"Since my first job was with the State in eminent domain cases I stayed in that specialty. But all through law school I had lofty ideals. Perhaps they came from my military experience. I thought I could make a contribution to world peace and civil rights."

"Why civil rights?"

"Because my Navy experience got me exposed to struggles some of my friends experienced. A few years ago, at the opening of the new YMCA in Oakland, Lionel Wilson said something that made me think."

"Lionel Wilson, the Mayor?"

"Yes. And I knew him as a judge. He described how, when he was a kid the blacks were not allowed in the downtown Y-that they had to go to the one in East Oakland. I thought-my God-I spent my whole youth at the Y downtown. I never noticed that. So it must be that when something doesn't affect a person that person doesn't notice it. In the Navy I heard about things that affected my friends, so then I understood."

"Examples?"

"One- when I was in New York waiting to be shipped to the Sixth Fleet, I had a lot of liberty time to spend in the City. By being in uniform people would come up to me and give me tickets to see the best shows in town. I was treated like a king. At the same time my friend Cruz Santos took the train to visit his mother in Arizona. He went into a restaurant-in uniform- and was told 'we don't serve Mexicans.' And that was in his home state! Another one-my friend Roscoe Adams was the best drummer I ever knew. He went into the Navy in 1949. Because he was black he had to be a steward-a servant to officers. Four years later they tried to get him to re-enlist. He made it a condition that he be sent to the Navy music school. So what I got immediately he had to wait four years to get, all because of his color."

"And did you lose those lofty ideals?"

"I did-by later events."

"What later events?"

"In law school I worked on the Kennedy campaign. Then came his assassination, then came the war in Vietnam, then came Robert Kennedy's assassination, then came Martin Luther King's. As my practice and my family occupied my time my ideals were forgotten-especially after we bought that house at Tahoe."

"Tell me more about your Navy experience."

"Well, at age eighteen the draft for the Korean War was on. I could have had a deferment by being in college, but I couldn't afford college. I thought I should get it over with to be able to get the GI Bill-it was about to expire. I heard that, if I could qualify as a Navy musician, I'd spend time at the Navy music school in Washington and then be sent to a Navy Band somewhere. I was sent to the Sixth Fleet Band. I played percussion and keyboards-usually accordion when a piano was not available. That was before the days of electronic keyboards."

"You couldn't afford college? Didn't your parents pay for that?"

"No, and I don't blame them. No one in my family had ever gone to college. My father graduated from high school and later became a CPA. My parents went through the depression. When I graduated from high school it was my turn to get a job."

"Your father was a CPA. How did he get his education?"

"During the second world war he studied accounting while at sea. When I was in the Navy he paid for me to take the same courses he took-by correspondence."

"How do you spend your time now?"

"I look for my glasses. I tried to keep up on the law, practice the piano, do some studying, but I didn't have the time or the place for those things. So, I spend my time looking for my glasses."

"What kind of a piano do you have to practice on?"

"It's a Steinway concert grand-old enough to be an antique. It left the factory in New York in 1871. I had it restored by a Steinway expert."

"1871! How does that piano compare with more modern ones?"

"By about 1890 Steinway perfected the grand piano. If the piano I had restored was a more modern Steinway, other things being equal, it would be a better and much different piano. But our piano has a charm that can't be duplicated. It also has a beautiful case that you don't see today."

"You mentioned your house at Tahoe. Do you still have it?"

"Regretfully, Yes. I'd like to sell it."

"Do you enjoy it?"

"I used to. That was some time ago."

"Isn't it a place for your leisure time?"

"There's never any leisure time there! We bring our work with us."

"How so?"

"We bring our computers. I bring printed music. Sarah brings her bank records and all kinds of other files. The whole time we're there we either work on the house or do the same work as at home-including the computer work. How I hate computers. If I only could have lived before computers came into the world."

"What about the snow? Do you go to your Tahoe house to ski?"

"I started skiing late in life. When we bought Tahoe I hoped to get better at it. As it turned out I never skied after that. Like a lot of things-I thought I'd play a lot of tennis up there. My old wooden racket is still on the wall there in the rec room-as a decoration."

"So you were disappointed with the house because you didn't get better at skiing and at playing tennis?"

"Maybe so."

"What about Sarah? Are there some things about the Tahoe house that are special to her?"

"She enjoys everything up there much more than I do now."

"Do you think about that when deciding whether to sell that house?"

"It bothers me. I don't want to disappoint her, as I do with everything else."

"About your piano-I play a bit myself. What's your preference-classical, jazz, solo, group?"

"I started with classical and I've stayed with it. When I began playing jazz it was solo. Being a Navy musician got me into playing with a group. We played a lot of jazz, especially in our spare time."

"How did your playing solo and playing jazz with a group differ?"

"It's much different with a group. It depends on what the group consists of. There's usually a drummer, so the piano player is freed from having to stress the beat. If there's a bass player it's important not to tread on his toes. So then I wouldn't use a walking bass line. With most groups the important role of the piano player is to feed the chord changes to the soloist. The voicing of those chords differs with the jazz era. But that's all behind me now."

Laying his pad and pencil on the desk Freidman said:

"So I think we've laid the groundwork today. What I want to discuss with you next time is my impression that you don't like your retirement, you don't like the way you spend your time and you don't like your house at Tahoe. How about next year on Wednesday, February 9 at 2:00 PM?"

John held back his thoughts. *I won't come back. This is a farce. I'll call next week to cancel.* He answered: *"That's fine."*

John now gone, Friedman wrote to Dr. Kern:

Thank you for referring Mr. Hayden to me. During my initial interview he demonstrated typical signs of depression. I hope more therapy will put him on the path to improvement.

On John's drive home his mind raced: *I don't need a* shrink. *What I need is to convince Sarah it's time to sell that God damned house. Then, I'll cancel with that guy.*

Chapter Twenty Two

Sarah answered the phone: "Hi Sarah, this is Marilyn".

Marilyn and Sarah were friends from childhood. As Marilyn and Jack live in Reno John and Sarah see them occasionally when they go to Tahoe.

"Marilyn, where are you?"

"We're in Danville. Jack came down to see his brother. Jim's in the hospital. He's OK now, but he had a slight heart attack. I thought I'd come see you while Jack stays here with Jim."

"Sure. That would be great. I'm here alone. John's at some doctor's office. Some doctor he thinks is going to fix his arthritis."

"Good. I'll be there in about twenty minutes."

When Marilyn arrived, the two ladies went to the patio to sit under the umbrella.

"So how's John?" Marilyn asked. "Did he recover completely from that stroke he had at Tahoe?"

"Yes, he got over that, but he has other problems."

"Oh, what?"

"He has the notion that his life will be better when he gets rid of things. I sometimes wonder if he wants to get rid of me."

"Oh no. I know him. He couldn't get along without you. But what does he want to get rid of?"

"You remember that statue we used to have over there? He sold that. Now he wants to sell our house at Tahoe. He says we don't use it anymore so it's not worth putting money into it. I tell him I don't like to be changing my life every time he gets a whim. He's been acting strange lately."

"How's that?"

"He mopes around. Doesn't talk much-remember how he used to talk and laugh. He either sits alone at his computer or takes long naps in the afternoon. We don't go out anymore. He hates the drive to Tahoe. Sometimes I'll try to start a conversation and he says nothing. Sorry to tell you this, but I feel that I have no one to talk to anymore. So how's Jack?"

Chapter Twenty Three

Before dinner John poured his nightly Scotch on the rocks. Sarah had her Manhattan as she prepared the gravy for the roast.

John opened with what he planned to say:

"Let's face it; time has come to sell the house at Tahoe."

"Like you sold the statue? Oh no! You're not going to do something like that again."

"Well, think of the money we've put into it. First was the down payment, then we bought the Audi with four wheel drive, then all the furniture, then the yearly expenses-including the property taxes. We should get that money out and begin enjoying life. You want to travel, you want to remodel this kitchen-let's get able to do those things."

"You wanted to buy that house as much as I did. You wanted to spend that money for that house. All the expenses since we could have paid if you hadn't retired-without asking me. If you still had your office we could afford it, just as we used to."

"I don't still have my office, and that was my fault. I thought I'd take a year's sabbatical. Then what happened? I had that stroke, all because of that house."

"Oh no. You can't blame your stroke on that house. You were taking that stuff for arthritis."

Sarah began to cry. John knew he turned what could have been an enjoyable evening into an argument. He hated to argue with Sarah, and he hated to hurt her, though he knew he usually did both. He changed the subject.

"All right. Let's talk about it some other time."

Chapter Twenty Four

"When we left last time," Freidman said, "we talked about things you don't like."

"My problem is arthritis, remember?"

"Do you take anything for your arthritis?"

"No. That's what caused me to have a stroke, remember?"

"There are medications available for the treatment of depression. How would you feel about taking one I might prescribe for you?"

"I wouldn't take it. I take Viagra only, and that's for pleasure, not treatment."

"I also noted last time that you said you *used* to be happily married. What did you mean by that?"

"For one thing-I want to sell that house at Tahoe, Sarah doesn't. She says she doesn't want me to take that away the way I took the statue from her."

"Anything else?"

"She doesn't say it, but I feel her resentment that I'm in her way all during the day."

"And that's because of the retirement that you don't like?"

"Sure."

"So let's talk about your retirement. Have you travelled?"

"We had a great trip to Europe before I closed my office-not since."

"About your house at Tahoe- I know a little about the area. Where is it up there?"

"It's on the east side of the lake, in Nevada. The subdivision is called 'Sky land.' It's between Highway 50 and the lake-you don't need to cross the highway to go from the house to the lake. The lake is a block down. There's a private beach down there for the whole community. On Skyland Drive, the street on the lake, there are large homes with their private beaches-some with piers .That's where Harrah's Villa was. He'd entertain the stars in his shows there-people like Sammy Davis and Liberace. Lisa Minnelli's house was on that street."

"So I assume that when you bought it you were quite enthused-right?"

"Yes. That was my mistake. When our boys were in school they'd ask: 'Why don't we have a place at Tahoe. Our friends do'. I assumed that we were just not as affluent as our kids' friends. Even though our kids were adults when we got the house, maybe I felt that we might finally measure up. I thought it would be a place for the family. I even expected someday to convey a one-third interest to each of our two sons. But Greg's family didn't use it-they never went there. Jeffrey and his wife liked it, but they moved to Idaho. A family house it was not."

"What other hopes did you have for the Tahoe house when you bought it?"

"At first, I thought it could help my music. I met a few musicians. One even had me sit in one night at a restaurant. But I realized I wouldn't play there for the same reason I don't play at home."

"What's that?"

"I want to spend my evenings with Sarah. There's nothing in it for her to sit there alone."

"Did you ever think of living there full time?"

"I did. I thought of the possibility of our selling the Piedmont house, buying a condo in some place like El Dorado Hills for the winter and living the rest of the year at Tahoe."

"What became of that idea?"

"I realized I much prefer the Bay Area. I can't understand anyone who moves from this area."

"As you sit here now, what are your main complaints about your house at Tahoe?"

"Financial and distance."

"What is it about the distance?"

"Early on I enjoyed the trips back and forth. Gradually they became a chore. The only way is to drive. Highway driving today, especially because of so many aggressive drivers, is a challenge for me."

"Is there anything you still enjoy about your Tahoe house?"

"I'm happy that it's worth more than we paid for it-but I'll only enjoy that when we sell it. I'll always enjoy the beauty of Lake Tahoe. But I don't have to own to enjoy that."

"Anything else there that's still special for you today?"

"Well-the recreation room downstairs gives me a place to call my own. There I have my computer stand, a pool table, a stereo, a TV and a piano."

"Oh-what kind of piano do you have there?"

"It's a Knabe upright with an Ampico player-vintage 1920 or thereabouts. It was given to me by our neighbors next door in Piedmont. I have a lot of Ampico rolls to go with it."

"Tell me about the rolls."

"Most of them came with the piano. I bought a few more. Ampico and DuoArt players could duplicate expression, the others couldn't. On that Knabe I can hear composers like Scott Joplin, George Gershwin, Paderewski and Rachmaninoff playing their own things. I can hear great pianists who made those rolls in about 1920-Adam Carroll, Victor Arden, Frank Milne-so many others."

"What is it about what you hear on those rolls that you especially like?"

"Well, I'm old enough to know the lyrics of those songs. To hear the music without hearing or thinking about the lyrics is not enough. Then, to duplicate what the song writers intended you need both the verse and the chorus. Because of their reliance on fake books few musicians now ever play the verse. You hear the verse on the rolls, and they stress the melody. Now the jazz format is to improvise away from the melody. But on the rolls, although the player may be doing fantastic things, the melody is always there."

"What other music do you listen to now?"

"Concerts- we go occasionally to the San Francisco Symphony and the Oakland East Bay Symphony-not as often as in the past. Jazz-we're lucky to have Yoshi's here. On the radio we listen to KPFA for classical and KCSM for Jazz. Do you remember KJAZ-FM 91?

"I do. That was a few years back."

"My father was the CPA for Pat Henry, the station's owner. KCSM follows his format pretty well."

"You mentioned fake books-do you use fake books?"

"Oh yes. I got the first one in about 1950."

"I've seen the recent ones. Tell me about that first one."

"There was a service to professional musicians called 'TuneDex". Every month they'd print new tunes on a 3 by 5 card-melody and chord only- copyrights paid. Sometime around 1950 someone got the idea to mimeograph those cards three on a page. That was the first fake book-about one thousand tunes. All illegal-no copyrights paid. Now publishers are doing something like that with copyrights paid."

"So that's what you have now?"

"Over the years I've gathered them all, including lead sheets I've written. Most of the fake books I use now are by me."

"How did you learn to play from a fake book?"

"At about age twelve my uncle, a professional musician, told my parents I should study with Frank Denke. He was the best known pianist and composer in the bay area. He was on the staff at NBC and the best musician ever in the Bohemian Club. From him I learned music theory and how to improvise. Reading the melody and chords and improvising the rest is called 'faking'. That's how we get the name 'fake book.'"

"So today, tell me why you like to play the piano."

"I like to play. I hate to practice. To practice I have to be alone. To play I need an audience. I never have an audience. My greatest insult is someone coming into my house and not asking me to play. I'm insulted constantly. The only people who come into our house are Sarah's friends. I don't have friends. Maybe her friends are not musical, or maybe I should take the hint."

"Maybe they don't know that you play the piano."

"Our Steinway concert grand is in our living room. Wouldn't you think someone would ask who plays it? Never."

"So do you think now that your arthritis hampers your playing?"

"It sure does."

"Does it affect your playing of both classical and popular?"

"Popular-far more."

"Why is that?"

"Long ago I was influenced by ragtime. That brought me to Harlem Stride- like Fats Waller. Then I went to swing with walking left hand tenths- like Teddy Wilson. That puts a lot of stress on the left thumb. Look-with our fingers we play on this pad opposite the nail. But we don't play on the pad on our thumbs, as if we were making a thumb print. Instead we play of this bone on the side. Without that pad to soften the blow the bone transfers the jolt down to that joint. There's much less of that stress in playing classical. I often thought I'd have to play classical only."

"So do you try to play around it?"

"Yes. I try a single note walking bass, or I try left hand voicing in close position. That's OK but not the way I want to play."

"What have you done so far to try to alleviate the problem with your thumbs?"

"Everything my doctor told me to do. First, a cortisone shot-painful but no help, Then he sent me to a therapist. I thought it was just to get thumb splint, but I had to get the full treatment-sitting there with a lot of old farts holding little vibrators on their aching joints. The fat chick calling herself a therapist showed me how to hold a pencil. I told her I do that quite well, thank you. Finally she gave me the splint that cost me $175.00. I threw that out."

"OK. Now, let's talk about music you like to hear-away from the piano. What's your liking in that situation?"

"The classics and the musical plays. I've always been interested in the American Musical Theatre."

"Tell me about what you like there."

"From opera and vaudeville we got the operettas. What great music from people like Rudolf Friml and Victor Herbert. Then we got the cute musicals with good songs but no plot. Those little shows from people like Rodgers and Hart and George Gershwin gave us the standards. Then came the revolution-*Show Boat,* with not only the magnificent music of Jerome Kern but also social comment-racial prejudice and inter-marriage. The trend continued with *Oklahoma* and *South Pacific* from Rodgers and Hammerstein. Now the musical theatre has come full circle, back to the opera mode, starting with Leonard Bernstein and *The West Side Story* and moving on to Andrew Lloyd Webber- I've seen all his things. With *Evita*- I'm old enough to remember hearing about Eva Peron. Who knows? Maybe that's where the Connollys got the name."

"The Connollys? Who are they?"

"People who once lived next door to us. They were our friends."

"Have you mentioned to any of your friends that you're in therapy?"

"God no! You call it that. I call it help for my arthritis-and, it isn't helping!"

"Are you ashamed to talk about that?"

"I don't talk about a lot of things."

"You like Rachmaninoff?"

"OK. Sure I know he saw a shrink. But let's talk about something important."

"So you like Andrew Lloyd Webber. I do too. I've seen *Phantom* twice. How often do you go to see the musicals?"

"You know about the Woodminster Summer Musicals up at Joaquin Miller Park in the Oakland hills?"

"Yes, I've been there."

"My father was the accountant for them. He and my mother would see every show. Sarah and I would usually go with them. We'd have a picnic in the park before the show or we'd go to Cesare's restaurant down the hill after."

"Do you still see those shows?"

"Not as often, but I see they're doing *Cats* next year. They've come into the big leagues enough now to do big productions like that."

"OK. Let's get back to your stroke. Tell me more about it."

"Like everything it was my fault. It was at our Tahoe house. I have this damn arthritis in my hands-also bad circulation-my hands are always cold, there especially. I heard that Ginkgo Biloba would help the circulation. So I was taking that, along with Aleve for the pain. On the morning of New Year's Eve my speech was garbled. Sarah took me to the hospital in South Lake Tahoe, they diagnosed it as a bleeding in the brain, and then I went by helicopter to the hospital in Reno. Because of the stroke I never went back to practicing law."

"So do you think your Tahoe house caused your stroke?"

"It wouldn't have happened down here."

"And now you hate that house because it caused your stroke?"

"It also caused me to lose my livelihood."

"Any results from that stroke still today?"

"My speech will never be the same."

"Getting back to music, did you stay with it after you left the Navy?"

"Not much. I was in college and I worked part time in my father's accounting office. But I was playing a solo gig for a fund raiser when a Judge came up and asked if I wanted to join his Dixieland band. I did".

"Was it all Dixieland?"

"Like Turk Murphy, we called it 'Traditional Jazz.' We played things like *Royal Garden Blues, See See Rider, Bill Bailey, Careless Love*-that type of thing."

"Still play with that group?"

"No. I gave it up. We were playing too frequently. Sarah would be sitting there with nothing to do. So they got another piano player and now they're the Bohemian Club's Jazz Band."

"Do you play with any other groups now?"

"No. I don't know anyone who plays."

"What about solo?"

"No more. Anyway, with this arthritis it's all over."

"For our next session, I'll be gone for a while. How about Wednesday, July the 20th at 2:00?"

John thought: *So I'll do this one more time and then tell him he's not helping my arthritis.*

Chapter Twenty Five

Friedman began: "At our last meeting you indicated that you don't like retirement. For most people that's their dream. Why not you?"

"I never wanted to retire and I hate that word." John answered. "After a financial disaster, I decided to take a sabbatical. I hoped to go back to work, but then I had the stroke."

"What was the financial disaster?"

"By spending too much time at Tahoe my clients went elsewhere. Then I lost my lease and my secretary. I gave up, telling myself I'd be back in a year. Then I had the stroke and lost my speech."

"After the stroke, and after your speech got better, why didn't you go back to work?"

"As you hear, my speech has not come back completely. And who wants to hire an old lawyer with health problems?"

"Tell me what you don't like about being retired?'

"Everything. When I was in my office I had some privacy. Now I have none."

"How so?"

"In my office I could close the door and think. Now, at home in that room off the kitchen Sarah's always there."

"Why are you in that room off the kitchen?"

"Our house dates back to the twenties. Then people in our area had maids. The typical maid's room and bathroom was adjacent to the kitchen. That maid's room became our son Greg's bedroom. His brother Jeff had the guest bedroom and bath upstairs. When I moved home from my office downtown I wanted to put the furniture I once had in my private office in what had been Jeff's bedroom upstairs. All my furniture would go into that room-my large desk, the matching credenza, the two side chairs, the couch-that room would have made a perfect office. I even thought that a part-time secretary could work in the maid's room downstairs. But Sarah said-and she was right-that we couldn't turn our house into an office. We needed the guest room upstairs for a guest we may have, and she hoped that our grandchildren would stay with us sometimes. So what had been my office furniture was spread around the house-the maid's room wouldn't accommodate it. In the maid's room I had to use the old roll-top desk Greg had."

"So while you're in that room Sarah is doing her work in the kitchen next to it, is that it?"

"That's it."

"And what difference does that make?"

"She's a multi-tasker-I guess most women are. She doesn't understand that I need concentration and continuity, so she talks to me every time she gets a thought, regardless of what I may be doing."

"You should realize, though, that you're not in your office anymore-You're in her world now."

"Exactly. I don't belong there. "

"Last time you mentioned the statue. You said something about taking it away from Sarah."

"I sold it."

"So you once had a statue and then you sold it. What kind of statue?"

"It was a life-sized lady lying nude in a hammock. It came from Italy to San Francisco for the 1915 Panama Pacific Exhibition. She was in our neighbors' yard. They called her 'Eva'. They were the Connollys-remember, I told you about them. By a fluke she ended up in our backyard."

"Sounds like quite a fluke. How did you get her?"

"The owner before the Connollys was a man named Keeley. He bought Eva at that Fair in 1915. She stayed in his yard when the Connollys bought the house from him. The Connollys sold the house to the Hogans and they sold the house to the Emersons. The Emersons said they didn't want her-they had a young girl they didn't want to be playing in a yard with a nude lady. So the Hogans offered her to us. We kept her for years in our back yard."

"How did you manage to sell her?"

"For that Sarah will never forgive me. Ever since we got Eva I tried to find out whether the story about her being at the1915 Panama thing was true. Then we had a chance to go to Florence. We actually found a gallery there named Frilli- that was the name stamped on Eva- down at her base. The person there spoke English. I showed her Eva's picture. She said she was beautiful, she said the stamp meant that she was from that gallery, but she said they had no records going back that far. She knew nothing about the1915 Panama Pacific Exhibition. She kept the picture and took down my name and address."

"So did she offer to buy it?"

"No. And I didn't say we wanted to sell her. I did ask how I might clean her. She said I'd need an expert for that."

"I still don't know how it was that you sold her."

"Sometime later we got a letter from the lady at Frilli Gallery. She enclosed a Sotheby's brochure showing a similar statue-the same statue, but in much better condition. It indicated that it sold for $575,000. On the brochure was the name of the dealer in Los Angeles who handled it. I called him. He came to look at Eva. He said she was in bad condition-she was, that he'd have to replace the missing part-I knew that, and that he'd have to send her away to be restored. Then he offered to buy her for $70,000. We finally agreed on $90,000."

"So you thought that was a good deal?"

"Yes. She had deteriorated a lot, we got her free and, to tell the truth, I thought it would make up for the money we had been putting into the house at Tahoe."

"And about that house at Tahoe, you told me about the room downstairs where you have the piano with the Ampico player. You don't have that at your Piedmont home, right?"

"Right."

"So that's something you can enjoy only at Tahoe?"

"Score one for you. That was good cross-examination of your adverse witness. If the shrink business gets bad the law school is there in Berkeley."

"I'll keep that in mind."

"Is there something else you still enjoy about Tahoe?"
"There's something else my dog-Riley- still enjoys."
"What's that?"
"Next to our subdivision is a large tract of US Forest land. We take him there to run and swim in the lake-Riley's a Golden Retriever."
"Pretty lucky dog."
"He doesn't have to pay for it."
"So your piano there is in that room downstairs."
"And also upstairs where I have the grand."
"You have a grand piano there too? Where did that come from?"
"I bought a Knabe grand that was restored by Sheldon Smith. By its serial number he found it was manufactured in 1918. I had it moved up to Tahoe.
"Sheldon Smith-That's a name I haven't heard before. Who is he?"
"Who was he? He was the piano technician who restored my Steinway. He became a good friend. He'd come by our house often, not only to tune the piano. One time he phoned at night, asking if he could bring a client by in the morning, He said he was restoring a piano like ours for this client and he wanted him to see ours. He told me the client's name. He said he was some kind of Rock Star. I said sure. The next morning he and the guy arrived just as I was leaving for the office. I told them to make themselves at home as I drove off. That night, at dinner, my sons asked the name of the Rock Star. I told them Sheldon said his name was Neil Young. The kids said: 'Dad, Neil Young was in our house and you didn't tell us.' I wonder now if Neil Young still has Sheldon's piano."
"Are you and Sheldon still friends?"
"Sheldon died after I sold Eva."
"Are you indicating that there was some connection?"
"I'll leave that up to you Freud guys."
"How did he die?"
"Suicide. He had many problems; I should have realized that."
"Do you think you added to his problems?"
"His big problem was with the bottle."
"It's often true that close friends blame themselves for a person's suicide. Do you have feelings along those lines?"

"Maybe I should have listened closer to his complaints. Maybe I should have spent more time with him, especially when I gave him lessons."

"Tell me about the lessons."

"He'd play a few bars of a few things-especially after he finished tuning. Either a Chopin Waltz or, his favorite, *In A Mist* by Bix Beiderbecke. He asked me to help him with jazz theory. Maybe I should have given him more time. I was at our house at Tahoe when he shot himself. If only I had been home that week."

"Is that another thing you blame on that house?"

"Maybe so."

"You and that house had nothing to do with his suicide. I've experienced enough of them to tell you that. Please remember that-You're in no way responsible for Sheldon's death."

"When his death was announced many famous pianists, like Peter Mintun, gave him tribute. On KPFA radio I played *In A Mist* as my memorial."

"OK-please remember what I just told you."

Putting his pen down Freidman said: "I see now that you like old things. I do too. Your 1871Steinway grand, your 1918 Knabe grand and your 1920 Knabe upright-that's quite a collection. Next time, let's concentrate on the statue-that's even older. Please bring whatever you have about the statue-photos or other things. I must tell you, I hear a lot of stories. But this one of yours about your statue has me intrigued. My secretary will call to make the appointment."

CHAPTER TWENTY SIX

"Let's talk about the statue and the 1915 Fair", Friedman said, starting the session. "Did you bring some photos?"

"I brought my file on it."

"Good. About the 1915 Fair, did you ever find out whether your statue came from there?"

"This you won't believe. About a year after we sold her a man who walks up our street was in front of our house when Sarah was there. He asked her 'What did you do with the statue? I used to see it through your window there in your back yard. It's not there anymore.' Sarah told him we sold it. Then he said 'It was from the 1915 Fair.' Sarah said: 'We heard that. How did you know?' He told her he was an antique dealer, that he had the brochure of the Frilli Gallery's items at the 1915 Fair, and that the statue's picture was in it. The next day he allowed me to make a copy of the brochure. So what I couldn't find out at the public library, what I couldn't find out by traveling to Florence to the Frilli Gallery, I finally found out by a man who walks up and down the street in front of our house!

Here are copies of pages from the Frilli brochure. See this first page has 'PPIE' at the top. That means Panama Pacific International Exposition. And you see 'Antonio Frilli' in the middle. It gives the address at '4 Via Dei Fossi' at the bottom-that's the address where we went in Florence. And look at this third page-a picture of Eva. She has the inscription 'Sweet Dreams'. Before I copied these pages I never knew that Eva's name was Sweet Dreams. It says she was 'designed by Prof. Albano' and 'executed by A. Frilli'."

"What did you do with that brochure?'

"I sent copies of those pages to the dealer who bought Eva from us-I guess I should have asked for some payment-I didn't. Next I saw he added that information to his ad trying to sell her."

"Did you find out whether he ever sold her?"

"His website just said she was sold. I don't know who bought her."

"What other photos are there in your file?"

"Here's a picture when she was still in our yard. See the broken piece by her feet?"

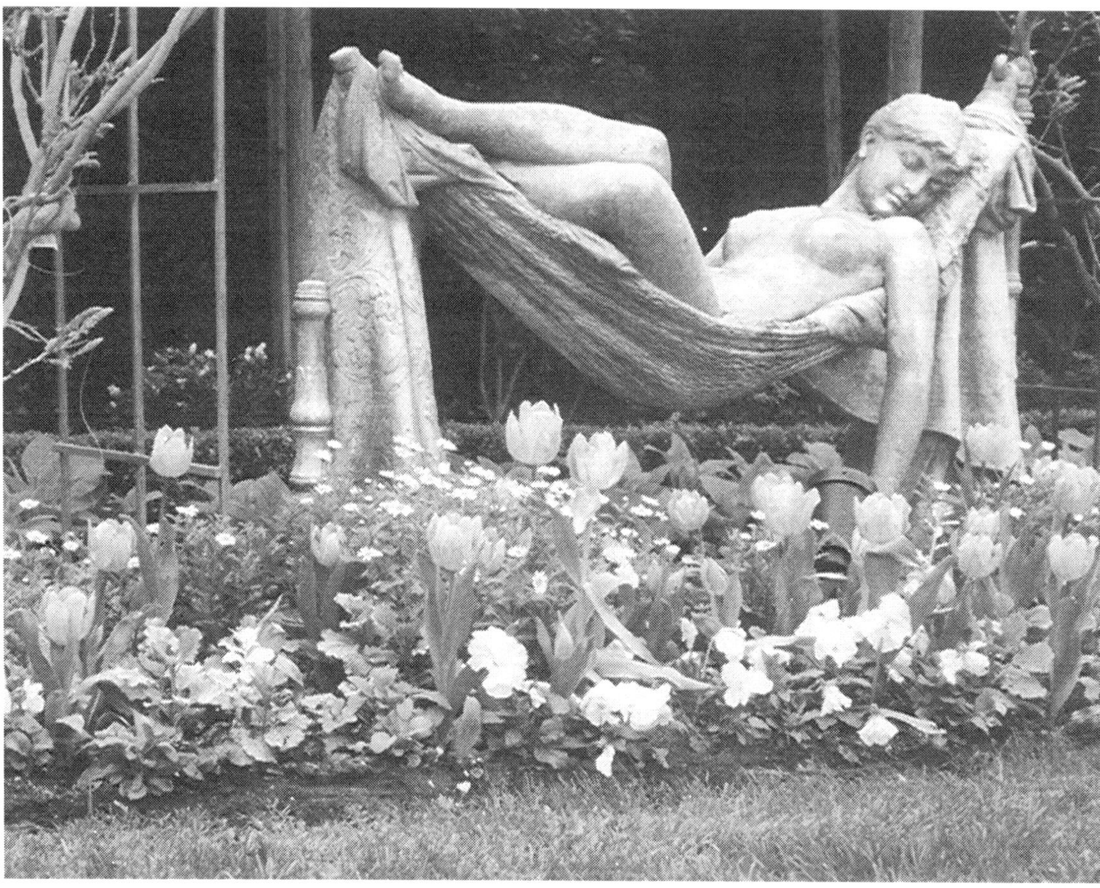

"So this statue gives you a lot of grief, does it?"

"She cursed me."

"She cursed you? How did she do that?"

"By sending her away."

"So these events you've told me about-these events that happened after you sold her-were all caused by her curse?"

"So it seems to me. Look-many years ago we were in Hawaii. At the volcano park on the big island my son Jeff grabbed a piece of lava. The guide said that Madame Pele would bring ten years of bad luck to anyone who took her lava. Jeff dropped it right there. Eva-she's my Madame Pele."

"Let me ask you to think like a lawyer. You told me about the Oakland Hills fire and how it destroyed your parents' home. Was that before or after the curse?"

"Before."

"And your father's murder. Before or after the curse?"

"Maybe you should try law school."

"Well, you see my point. Adversities happen to all of us. Is that curse just your scapegoat?"

"Think what you want. I'm still trying to replace her."

"Did you try to find something that would do that?"

"I did and I still do. I go on line every day looking for garden stoneware and statuary. I find nothing like it. When I do find something even approaching it, it's far too expensive. I thought I might be able to afford something by selling my Steinway."

"What about the pianos at Tahoe?"

"I'd sell them too, but all three pianos wouldn't bring enough to replace Eva."

"What would Sarah think about you selling your Steinway?"

"That's another problem. She doesn't want to part with anything, not even with a piano she doesn't play."

"I think we need a few more discussions on other things, though. Next time let's talk about some solutions you may not have considered."

"Wait a minute! I've been having these sessions with you long enough. I think they should end right here. At least, let's put it off for a while. Let me decide if I want to talk to you again."

"That's fine. Perhaps you should do just that. Spend that time thinking about what we've been over. See if you can resolve these things on your own. Then, if you want to talk to me again, you know I'm here."

CHAPTER TWENTY SEVEN

Four years passed. John continued trying to hide his depression. Sarah knew better.

Something new did happen. Graham Carter, publisher of the Piedmont Courier, recommended John's piano playing for the 2009 Piedmont Jazz Festival. As John thought his playing there was not up to his standards, he was convinced to call for another session with Freidman. It would be on December 15.

"So I see it's your birthday today", Freidman began. "Happy birthday."

"They're coming all too fast these days. Time is one of the many things I can't control."

"Let's talk about time. During these years I haven't seen you have you spent some time practicing the piano?"

"Some time, yes. The best time is in the morning while Sarah is still sleeping, though I seldom do it. My practicing, as with other things that don't involve her, is a thorn sticking into our marriage."

"Why is that?"

"What other man, retired and in his seventies, has the job of practicing the piano two or three hours a day? I try to keep up with French. That takes time. What other man does that? At one time I even tried to write a novel. That took time. All this time would be better spent if I did things she'd like to do. We have married friends where the men have no time demands. They can do the things their wives want them to do. I can't, all because of the stupid demands I put on my own time."

"If you gave up the piano, if you forgot about French, if you never try to write, if you, as you say, would be like other men you know-would you be happier?"

"I'll cross that bridge when, or if, I come to it."

"About your piano, have you ever thought of recording some of your playing?"

"I did. About three years ago my friend set up equipment for me to record on digital tape. He then transferred that onto his computer to make CDs. That gave me three CDs of the standards and one of the classics. He put fancy labels on them so they could be sold."

"Sounds like a good friend. Is he still?"

"He was-until he died last year-brain cancer."

"What did you do with the CDs?"

"I sent them to a company that sells CDs to the public-It's called *CD Baby*. But first I got copyright licenses."

"Just like a lawyer. How did you go about that?"

"There's a service called the *Harry Fox Agency*. It makes the process easy. For the classics I didn't need to pay for copyrights-those I chose were in the public domain. For the standards the charge for each tune wasn't much. And for the CDs it was based on the number of CDs sold. I knew I wouldn't sell that many, so my one charge was all."

"Did they sell?"

"A few, mainly through my website."

"Oh! You have a website?"

"Yes, through CD Baby. My son Jeffrey designed it-he's my webmaster."

"So all your friends go to your website I imagine."

"Are you kidding? No one has ever told me they went to my website. On my telephone answering machine I asked people to see my website. On my business card and my email signature I have it listed. No one has ever indicated that they've seen it."

"Why don't you tell them to see it?"

"I never want to force anyone to do something that has to do with me. Like playing the piano, I prefer that they ask me to do it."

"So, how did your CDs sell through your website if your friends didn't go there?"

"They didn't sell to my friends. I made the mistake of giving my CDs to them. But, perfect strangers would either trip over my website, or they would go to CD baby and browse my type of thing."

"About those CDs, would you consider bringing copies to me next time?"

"I'll mail them to you. God knows whether they'll get here."

"I'd be most grateful to get them. Speaking of God, how do you feel now about religion? You're Catholic. How do you feel about the Catholic religion?"

"In four years of Catholic high school I was steeped in it. My doubts came later. The church stood in the way of science when it condemned Galileo. The church told us that the only excuse for sex was procreation-so no birth control. Priests were to be celibate. So we have some priests who are deviates. Women couldn't be priests. If the church ever comes to its senses, priests will be allowed to marry and women will be allowed to be priests."

"Do you think that it's celibacy that causes some priests to be, as you say, deviates?"

"If they were allowed to be normal, more normal men would choose to be priests."

"Have you ever experienced abuse by priests?"

"Never. In four years of Catholic high school I was taught by the brothers. They were strict, good teachers, very dedicated and never abusive."

"You went to Catholic schools. Did you send your sons to Catholic schools?"

"No. We have excellent schools in Piedmont, so they had no reason to go to Catholic schools to get a better education."

"How about Sarah? Is she still a practicing Catholic?"

"Oh, yes. I go to church with her, just to be with her. Now, we have a big church event coming up. I hope I can go along with all the ritual."

"What's the big church event?"

"Next year, on January 30^{th,} it will be our fiftieth anniversary. We'll have a Mass and reception at our home for more than 100 people. Our sons and grandchildren will be involved in the church and home ceremonies."

"So are you looking forward to your anniversary?"

"The party part will be OK. I'll try to look sincere during the Mass."

"Will you take a trip after the event?"

"No. Nothing planned now."

"My wife and I went on a cruise. Twelve days, through the Mediterranean. You told me you spent some time at sea-and at the Med. Have you considered taking Sarah on a cruise?"

"I might. There is something relaxing about being at sea. She's never experienced that, maybe she should."

"I'd recommend that. Now, let's get back to solutions. What's your exercise routine?"

"When I had my office I'd go at least three times a week to the Oakland Athletic Club-not only to keep in shape but also to be with my friends. That's gone".

"There are clubs like that now."

"Not the same."

"What about your law practice-isn't something left there?"

"Not since my stroke. Last year I completed a two week course in mediation, I renewed my membership in the local bar associations and got my name on the court panels for mediators. But I don't have an office and I haven't had any requests to mediate."

"Maybe you could borrow an office."

"No way! All you're giving me is a lot of wishful thinking."

"What's wrong with wishful thinking? You know, some people call that prayer. Maybe you should try it. Now, what about your music? How about donating your services to some of the old folks' homes around here?"

"I'd rather play for young people-I'm tired of being with old farts like me."

Freidman had enough. "I must say, Mr. Hayden, I'm tired of hearing your excuses. It seems to me that you're the guy they had in mind when they said 'be careful what you wish for.' You have what most guys wish for-A loving wife, a home in Piedmont, a second home at Lake Tahoe, grown children, grandchildren, retirement and good health- and yet you're depressed! What I suggest is that you take the initiative to restore the opportunities you once had. What do I mean by that? You must have taken the initiative a long time ago to advance yourself as a lawyer. Do that again. So you want to be a mediator. Take the initiative to contact some other lawyers to let them know you're available. So you want to play piano in public. Take the initiative to let people know you do. So you want people to visit your website. Take the initiative to let them know about it. Yes, you are an extrovert, but you've been hiding it. Take the initiative to be that again. It may be too late for you to tap dance at the world's fair, but you can still play music and sing. Go ahead and be the show-off you once were. And, you remember the exercises the speech therapist gave you. I'm sure you can think of others. Take the initiative to do those exercises again. There's no excuse for you to be self-conscious about your speech. And, I'm tired of hearing your complaints about your house at Tahoe. Take the initiative there- try to go there without your computer. Try to be there without having to practice the piano. See if Sarah can go there without her work. Then, ask yourself, what do the tourists do up here? What do others who have second homes do? See if there's something up there for the both of you without bringing your work and worries with you. Do that before you decide to sell or when to sell. And about that curse, we all try to find something or someone to blame for our troubles. Take the initiative to convince yourself that the curse is only your mind's way to find an excuse for not thinking as you-a lawyer-should. And one more thing, you've told me a lot of good things about your sons-you're proud of them. But have you told them you are? It's OK for a man to tell his adult son he loves him. Have you told them that? Just take the initiative-do that."

John felt he should respond in kind. But it had been a long time since someone had balled him out. Somehow, that evoked a happy memory.

"So," Freidman said, regaining his composure, "your anniversary is next year on January 30. Why don't we meet on April 9th? How about 3:00?"

"OK for now. I may have to call you if things change."

"That's fine. And- happy anniversary!"

CHAPTER TWENTY EIGHT

It was a sunny day. The event went as Sarah had planned-much better than John expected. Father Leo, the Pastor at Corpus Christi, said the Mass. Sarah saw to it that Father John was invited. He was the Pastor at Our Lady of Tahoe, the little church tucked into the trees at Zephyr Cove by their Tahoe house. He made the trip down to Piedmont to con-celebrate the Mass with Father Leo.

At Sarah's direction, the men in the ceremony were dressed in tuxedos. The women wore their best gowns. Sarah was beautiful in hers. The granddaughters were the bridesmaids. Gregory and Jeffrey gave the readings, and John and Sarah renewed their vows.

Something about the ritual struck a familiar note in John's mind. Could it be that the religious indoctrination of his youth remained less than dormant? Or was it the sermon by Father Leo- all about how God loves his creations and brings lovers like John and Sarah together? Or was it Corpus Christi itself? John couldn't deny the coincidences- that he met her at that church, that they were married there, that their boys received the sacraments there and that their parents' Funeral Masses were held there. Or, could it have been that Father John explained how the couple came to his little church at Tahoe and how Sarah's enthusiasm for life gave it a new breath? When it came time for the two to kiss after Fathers Leo and

John pronounced them "man and wife," John tried to hold back a tear. *What's happening here?* He thought. *Is this ritual really getting to me? I'll try not to show it.*

Jeffrey drove them home. He said to John:

"You seemed a bit moved, Dad."

"Just part of the process". John answered. He couldn't be truthful and felt he didn't have time to think of a more witty response.

CHAPTER TWENTY NINE

"What a wonderful party, Sarah", Barbara said. She and Sarah had been friends since childhood. "And your boys- how I loved that reading by Jeffrey."

"You know he's quite popular at his church", Sarah bragged. "He's the assistant pastor there."

"Then that reading by Greg! Everyone laughed after he read the Irish Greeting. Was he supposed to say the word of the Irish?"

"No. He always wants a laugh. He was supposed to say the word of the lord."

"Sarah -those girls! How beautiful! The two are so grown up!"

"Yes. They're Greg and Michelle's girls. The younger two are Jeffrey and Kathleen's girls. We love them all."

"Well, Sarah I'm sorry we haven't seen each other in so many years. I guess the last time Angelo and I were here John had his office in the Breuner building. Is he still practicing?"

"No. He retired."

"So you must be having lots of fun now."

"Yes and no."

"What present did John give you for your fiftieth?"

"He says he's trying to find something just right."

"Well, the church was beautiful and Father Leo's sermon made me cry. I think I may have seen a tear in John's eye too. And your home-there were tables for everyone!"

"Thanks to the weather people could be in the garden."

"Oh, yes, Sarah. That reminds me what I wanted to ask you. The last time we were here you had the sleeping lady statue under the archway back there. What happened to it?"

"Well, that's a sore subject. We've been without her for a few years now. John wanted to sell her."

"Oh! I'm sorry Sarah. But let's try to get together more often."

CHAPTER THIRTY

The anniversary was more than a month ago. John was back to his old routine. As Sarah slept he searched the internet. On previous attempts, he had exhausted "statuary", "stoneware," and "garden art." *Our anniversary's over and I still haven't found a gift for her. If only I could find a substitute for Eva. OK Friedman, I'll "take the initiative"- I'll try again.* He tried something new. This time he typed "*Nude Sleeping in a Hammock.*" Scrolling beyond the porn sites he came to one about an "art exhibit."

What? An art exhibit? What kind of art exhibit would have the title "Nude sleeping in a hammock"? Click on this. What? The nineteenth century art collection of Andrew Lloyd Webber? Paintings and sculptures? Click on sculptures. What? My God! There she is! Eva! Could it be her? But there were others like Eva. It must be one of those. But, my God, it could be her! Does Andrew Lloyd Webber now own Eva? Andrew Lloyd Webber! How can this be? This is something I can't tell Sarah.

John spent a few more mornings on the internet. *If Andrew Lloyd Webber now owns Eva that's unbelievable! But it doesn't tell me what I can give to Sarah for our anniversary.*

Back to statues-sculptures and gardens-endless scrolling. *Oh! Wait a minute! Here's a statue. Not her but pretty close! Yes-a nude sleeping in a hammock. Beautiful!*

Looking closer John could see that this statue was a reproduction of Eva. The position of her face and feet were opposite from Eva's. It was smaller, but it looked new. It was pure white-no pits, no age spots. The sales pitch gave the name of the dealer in London and said that the statue was Carrara marble. It certainly looked as if that were true, but how could it be? Especially since the price listed was only $8,000. *For that I wouldn't have to sell the Steinway.*

John still had Gloria's phone number at the Frilli Gallery in Florence. Although it was 6:30 PM there, Gloria answered.

"This is John Hayden, Gloria. I hope you remember me and our sleeping nude statue."

"Yes, John, how are you and Sarah?"

"We're fine, Gloria. I know it's late where you are, but I've just come across something. Maybe you can solve my mystery."

"I can try."

"Gloria, I've just learned that a statue like ours is now owned by Andrew Lloyd Webber. Did you know that?"

"No. Do you think it's the one you had?"

"I don't know-that's a mystery I'd like to solve. And here's another thing: There's a reproduction of our statue for sale by a dealer in London. It looks perfect, but it's smaller and has fewer detailed carvings. It says it's Carrara marble. The price is only $8,000."

"Oh, but be careful. If a statue like that is on exhibit, especially if it's owned by someone famous, there will be copies made. A lot of copied statues are coming out of Asia."

"But Gloria I've got to tell you. Ever since we sold Eva, Sarah has been grieving. I've looked everywhere for a substitute, never expecting to find anything like her. Now, this seems to be a Godsend."

"I'm happy for you, John. Just be careful. Let me know what you do."

Just as John put the phone down it rang. *Was Gloria calling back?*

"Hello," John answered.

"Hello Mr. Hayden. I'm Fred Stanley calling you from Boalt Hall. How are you today?"

John thought: *What a time for a fund-raising call from Boalt Hall*!

"I'm fine, Fred. But I'm quite busy at the moment."

"I'll just be a minute, Mr. Hayden. I'm in charge of the Moot Court program. Thank you for participating as a judge in the past.

I noticed that it's been a while since we called on you. We have some interesting cases coming up. We're hoping that you'll help us again. May I send you the briefs?"

John hesitated. He couldn't grasp what had been happening this morning.

"Sure, Fred. I'd be happy to act as judge again. Send the briefs and give my regards to anyone who may remember me."

Back to the statue, John had the name of the dealer in London-Jonathon Smithson Antiques. He thought: *I'll take Freidman up on that 'take the initiative' thing. It's too late to call London now. I'll send an email to this guy and call him in the morning. I've got to see if I can get that statue in our yard. My God, wouldn't Sarah love that!*

Morning came. The call was made.

"I bought it from a dealer in Rome." Jonathon said. "She couldn't tell me how old it was. She said it was old, but it looked new to me. I bought it because it was such a beautiful piece. I can vouch for the fact that it is made of Carrara marble."

"What about the shipping cost?" John asked.

"That's always on the buyer," Jonathon answered.

"We're in Piedmont, California. Can you find what it would cost to ship the statue here?"

"Yes. I have your email. It should take me a few hours. I'll email that to you."

The email from Jonathon told John the shipping cost would be $1,500.00. The process should take 2 or 3 months, depending on the time needed for it to clear customs in New York. Jonathon accepted John's credit card. *Thank God! I think I bought her anniversary present!*

CHAPTER THIRTY ONE

"You seem a little brighter." Freidman said. "A stroke of good luck?"

"Maybe it's the weather."

"How did your anniversary go?"

"Very well. The weather cooperated. Everyone seemed pleased-we had more than one hundred people."

"And the Mass?"

"It went well. The whole family was involved."

"We've talked before about religion and your faith, or lack thereof. Was there anything about the anniversary that may have changed your viewpoint?"

"Well, maybe. But I'll leave religion to people in religion. Remember-I'm here about my arthritis."

"John, I hope to think that the sessions we've been having have been to your benefit. Your attitude today makes me think that may be the case."

"Not to disappoint you, but, maybe as I said before, it's just the weather."

"Here's an observation of mine-you may not agree-but I notice that today you're less of a pill. You even seem to talk like an ordinary guy who has something to live for."

"Well, I do like good weather."

"Do you agree that you seem a little happier?"

"Maybe that's because I'm trying to get along better with Sarah."

"That's a good reason."

"Maybe I'm trying to be a little more ordinary. But-please keep this confidential. A few things are in transition."

"Tell me about them."

"The miracle of the internet! I found that Andrew Lloyd Webber has an exhibit in London with a statue like Eva. It may not be her, but it is an exact duplicate."

"Did it tell you how much he paid for it?"

"No, and I don't care. His statue could be the one that was sold by Sotheby's for $575,000. It looked perfect on the internet, so I assume he paid something like that for it."

"How does that make you feel?"

"If it is Eva I'm happy she's not in some glitzy hotel in Las Vegas. And, I'm happy she's owned by an artist-someone who shares his art with the public. If it's not her, at least I know now that she's getting the respect she deserves."

"Is there something else in transition?"

"Yes. I found a reproduction of Eva for sale in London-also on the internet. I contacted the seller and ended up buying it. It's being transported through New York. Sarah doesn't know about it. It will be my present to her, and I didn't have to sell the Steinway to pay for it."

"Well! Was there any action on your part to cause these events?"

"Don't give me that 'take the initiative' bull shit. Maybe it's about time for my luck to change."

"Getting back to exercise: You told me how you used the Oakland Athletic Club. I do the same at the Berkeley Athletic Club. You're an old Blue-I think you'd like it. I'd be happy to sponsor you for membership."

"Well, I may go there sometime and see if I could work it in. I doubt it, but maybe."

"OK. Now let's talk more about your anniversary and the Mass. Was there something about it that improved your attitude about the Catholic Church?"

"Well, I'm always encouraged to see that we still have priests like Father Leo-the pastor of Corpus Christi, and Father John-our pastor at Tahoe."

"You say 'our pastor at Tahoe.' So you're now thinking of Tahoe as your home?"

"Not as home, but the little church there is very picturesque, with its window the full width behind the altar and all Tahoe's glory shining through."

"Tahoe is a glorious place, isn't it?"

"I'll admit that."

"OK. Now again about your piano playing: I got your CDs-thank you. I think your playing is much better than I could have expected from listening to you talk about it. I especially like the one named *Background Music* where you play all classical things-a lot of Chopin and Debussy. That Nocturne by Chopin-wasn't that used as a theme-song by someone?

"Yes-by Eddie Duchin. You must be older than you look."

"And what about that Chopin piece-what is it?

Berceuse?"

"That's Chopin's idea of a cradle song. I think of it as saying 'Sweet dreams.' "

"So does that piece make you think of Eva?"

"Yes-and you know-maybe you're right. Maybe I am a bit brighter today. Thinking of Eva used to make me sad. Now I guess I'm thinking of that new statue that will replace her. I'll call that one 'Evita'."

I read the insides of your CD covers. On the one for *Love is here to stay* you write: 'Ira Gershwin was able to write these brilliant lyrics: *In time the Rockies may crumble, Gibraltar may tumble, they're only made of clay*. Theologians never described eternity more succinctly.' First, let me share your admiration for the poetry of Ira Gershwin. But next, your words there bring us back to religion. Are you familiar with theologians?"

"Well, I've told you about religion in my life. Coincidentally, my son Jeffrey is on his way to being a theologian."

"I guess we share exposure to theology. I guess I had as much to learn in making my Bar Mitzvah as you in making your Confirmation. Okay, let's get back to your CDs. That piano has a beautiful tone. Did you record these CDs playing your Steinway?"

'I did."

"Well, you told me about Sheldon Smith. He certainly did a good job on your Steinway. Now, about your arthritis-you told me that it was mainly in your left thumb. You told me how you developed the stride and swing bass style and how your choices were to continue playing that way, develop a different way or give up playing entirely."

"I'm developing a different way. Not easy, but I'm doing it."

"What's the different way?"

"Since the problem is primarily the way I play the standards, I'm concentrating more on the classics."

"How does that help?"

"Fewer left hand tenths. For the octaves I play single notes. You know the descending octaves in the middle of the Chopin Polonaise-I play them as single notes."

"So you change the classics?"

"Yes, and who cares? When I hoped to play professionally, I had to toe the line. But now instead of giving it up I simplify things, and no one knows or cares."

"And how about the standards?"

"That's a more difficult change, but I'm working on it. I'm substituting single notes for octaves and tenths, playing a walking bass and getting used to a thinner sound. Again, it's better than giving it up."

"Well, I told you, remember, that I too dabble in music. In fact, I play once a week at a club in Marin County with a small group. We play some Dixieland, some modern jazz, but we mostly play swing. Can I induce you to sit in with us?"

"There you go again with that 'take the initiative' baloney. But it won't work. You're on piano! I know they can't have two pianos there."

"Well, I'm happy that I've been upgraded to baloney! They don't have two pianos there, but with this group, I play string bass. With me are Harold Lambing on drums, Chuck Diaz on trombone, Steve Fisher on guitar and George Breschi on tenor sax. Steve and Gene are lawyers. You may know them. It'll be nice to have a piano with us. Remember, you don't have to worry about the bass line- I'll try to do that. Lambing will provide the beat. Just give us the chord changes. If you want to solo or sing-that's up to you."

"Well, maybe. May I bring Sarah with me?"

"Sure. We all bring our wives. We have dinner on the house. Beer and wine included. We have a great time. The place is called The Green River Club."

"The old Dixieland tune: 'I had to drink the old green river dry to come back home to you.' Did you know that 'Green River' was a brand of whiskey?"

"Oh, yes. That's where the name comes from. OK. The Green River Club is on Lincoln Avenue in Mill Valley. Everyone around there can direct you. We start playing Thursday at 8."

"I'll have to think about it. I'll ask Sarah about it".

Seeming to disregard John's excuses, Freidman ended the session:

"I'll tell the guys that you'll be sitting in with us."

Chapter Thirty Two

The Contra Costa County Bar Association's annual list of members came in the mail. Seeing Dan Lilly's photo John thought he'd give him a call. *Not to take Freidman's initiative but to see how Jim Noonan is.*

"Hello Dan, this is John Hayden. Remember me?"

"Sure, John. How are you?"

"I'm fine. I was wondering how Jim was doing."

"He's enjoying his retirement. He's still in good health, keeping up with his exercise routine. You know, John, he often talks about you. He says you were the best of the lawyers he trained."

"Well, guys his age-and that includes me-get confused at times."

"By the way, John, I'm glad you called. I see your name in the court's list of mediators. I have a case heading that way. Could you hear it? The State's the plaintiff. Any conflict?"

"No conflict. When do you expect it to come to mediation?"

"A week from Friday. We're supposed to start at 10 AM."

"Well, I can do it then, but soon after that we're flying to Spokane to see our son Jeffrey. You think two days will do?"

"Oh sure. Where can we come to you?"

"I prefer not to hear these things at my house. Let me see if I can arrange a conference room and I'll get back to you."

John asked himself *why did I say I'd get a conference room?*

Bob Barton, a real estate broker, had been a friend and client of Ray Hayden. John had inherited his father's share in a limited partnership run by Barton. Barton's real estate office was on Grand Avenue. John thought: *So I'll try taking the initiative again*! Barton answered John's request: "Sure, John. You can use our conference room for that."

John couldn't believe what was happening. Maybe Freidman was right.

Yesterday's Piedmont Courier was on John's desk. He read the article about how the City had purchased the old Christian Science reading room. A group of citizens took over its management to make it a cultural arts center. They even purchased a Steinway B from Piedmont Piano Company, as they planned to hold small concerts there. *Why not give it a try, if only to show Friedman he's wrong!* John called the number listed at the article's end.

"Piedmont Arts Center". It was a pleasant female voice.

"Hello. This is John Hayden. I live in Piedmont and I'm interested in your arts center."

"Why hello Mr. Hayden. I'm Robin O'Neil. Do you remember me? I came to your home to interview you when I was with the Courier".

"Oh, Robin. Of course. And you're still here in Piedmont."

"Yes. I do volunteer work for The Arts Center. Do you still play the piano? We're looking for someone to play here."

"Well, thanks for remembering. I still play, and I'd be happy to play there."

Robin thought: *He's not so cranky now. Now he sounds half human. Maybe he was just having a bad day back then*. She said: "I'm writing that down Mr. Hayden. We'll be calling you."

"And Robin", John answered, "I hope you know I'm joking when I say: Have a nice, like, day."

"I remember that, Mr. Hayden, and I will. You too."

CHAPTER THIRTY THREE

John decided to *take the initiative* in a big way. He'd again talk to Sarah about selling that house.

What should I say to start? That we put too much of our money into that house? That we should have that money back for our future? No-I've told her that before. That the house caused me to lose my practice and to have a stroke? No. She wouldn't agree. OK, Freidman-I'll take the initiative. I'll just say that time has come. I'll try to talk nicer this time, but that's how I'll start.

As usual, they sat down for cocktails before dinner. Sarah poured her Manhattan and John's Scotch. John began:

"Look, Hon," John said," I know this is a difficult subject, but we must face it-time has come to list Tahoe for sale. We shouldn't be in a hurry to sell it, but we should get started. Selling it and moving our stuff out may be a long process."

"I know." Sarah said. "I can face up to that now."

John thought: *All these years I've been worrying about whether she'd agree to sell that house and now she agrees without an argument. Maybe Friedman was right. I should have tried a long time ago to be more reasonable in the way I talk to her.*

"But there's no need to hurry." John said. "We can put it on the market this year or next-it will probably take a while to find the right buyer. We can enjoy it in the meantime."

"Will you enjoy it?" Sarah asked.

"Sure. I do enjoy the pianos up there."

Chapter Thirty Four

Gregory came to drive them to the airport for their trip to see Jeffrey at Coeur d'Alene. With Sarah and Michelle in the back seat John talked to his son.

"We've decided to sell Tahoe. It may take a year or more. Before we do I hope that you'll have time to use it."

"That's good Dad. We'll remember that if we ever get some time off."

"And thanks for watching Riley while we're gone. He loves his meals and his walks around town. Otherwise he's happy to sleep."

"Sure, Dad. We'll take care of him. We're here at the Southwest Airlines curb. Have a good trip."

Greg opened the car's trunk and put the suitcases on the curb. After her kisses and hugs Sarah stood by the suitcases while John went back to talk to his son, now behind the wheel and ready to depart within the allowed time.

"Greg", John said in a low voice, "I want you to know I'm proud of you. Your professional accomplishments and your role as a father give you a star billing. You've kept up all these years with rowing- a lot of time and conditioning. You're in better shape than I ever was. And you've found the time to excel in all these things. Just remember, like your mother, I love you too."

"Thanks, Dad. That means a lot to me. I love you too."

The flight from Oakland to Spokane was uneventful. Jeffrey was waiting for them at the airport.

"Why the briefcase, Dad?" Jeffrey asked. "Looking for some Idaho cases?"

"No-I'm not ready to go back into the pits. I'm to be a judge at Boalt. They sent some briefs to read over. I guess they've gone into the archives to find some senior citizens."

John was surprised that the drive from Spokane to Coeur d'Alene was so short. After loves, kisses and settling down they were ready to gather around Jeffrey's barbecue.

"Come with me to take Bella for her walk, Dad", Kathleen said to John. "Jeffrey and Mom can stay here while he tends the barbecue."

"How's Riley doing?" Kathleen asked.

"He's fine. Greg and Michelle are watching him, at our house."

The coals were as Jeffrey preferred for barbecuing tri-tips. Kathleen and John were out of site.

"So how's he doing? Still going to the shrink?" Jeffrey asked.

"He's doing much better, but don't tell him about our telephone conversations. He thinks I don't know his Doctor Freidman is a shrink. He calls him his arthritis doctor."

"So why do you think he's doing better?"

"It's just something I noticed lately. His attitude seems much better. He practices the piano more-he gets up early to do it. He told me he'll be a judge at Boalt this year. He hasn't done that for a while. And, remember how he used to go to the Athletic Club-well, he's doing that again-in Berkeley. And, after he took that course to become a mediator he did nothing about it. Well, last week he did one. He always told me he couldn't do it without an office. But now he's arranged to use Bob Barton's office. And I think he's working on his speech again. It seems to me that he flubs his words less lately. He sure laughs more than he has for a long time. And last Thursday night he did something I thought he'd never do again."

"Oh Mom! Please don't tell me about your sex life."

"No, Jeffrey. What he did Thursday night was to play with a small band."

"Really! That's great news. How did that happen?"

"He told me his arthritis doctor invited him to play with a group over in Mill Valley. When we got there I met his Doctor Freidman. Dad's pretty dumb if he thought I couldn't tell this guy was a psychiatrist. He had a beard, he was chewing on a pipe, and he wore a tweed coat with leather patches on the sleeves-the whole nine yards. But they played really well. Dad even sang *After You've Gone* and told his old joke that it was named after a brand of toilet paper. Then he announced: 'ladies and gentlemen, now the tune sung by Marie Antoinette after the French Revolution- *I ain't got no-body.*"

"Well! It sounds like he's getting back to his old self."

"The latest is the Piedmont Arts Center. He tells me the young girl named Robin who interviewed him last year asked him to play there once in a while. He'll be playing there for some kind of thing in two weeks. He gave them copies of his CDs for them to sell for fund raising."

"How about Tahoe? Do you think he might start enjoying that more?"

"Would you believe-the last time there he didn't bring his computer. He asked me not to bring so much work. He played the pianos up there but he didn't practice. And, you know, he seemed to be having fun. I sure did."

"So how do you feel about this progress of his?"

"Jeffrey, my dear, I have to tell you-I'm so relieved. For all these years now he's been moping around the house. Now he gets out once in a while. I like him home, but now that he's not constantly in my hair--Oh-Here they come-let's change the subject."

Jeffrey's barbecue was an early dinner for John and Sarah, but with the warm evening and their joy at being with their kids and grandkids the evening was like old times.

"I'm working on my theology studies, Dad," Jeffrey said," how about a session with you tomorrow going over some of the religion we used to argue about?"

"It's a deal," John answered.

Chapter Thirty Five

In Jeffrey's boat on the lake John opened the conversation: "Looking at those hills, the trees, and this lake would make an atheist wonder."

"About those atheists, what about you, Dad? Still an agnostic?"

"Well there comes a time when the intellect may lead away from dogma."

"Come on, Dad. Where's religion in your life now? You've had some tragedies. How do you square that with a belief in God?"

"The theory is that God gave man free will, and that might do harm at times. I try to believe that, but it sometimes gets hard."

"Like Grandpa's murder. Did you still believe in God after that?"

"It was difficult. But, I'll admit that something inside tells me that God not only exists but that he, or she, wishes us well, despite how we may mess up our lives."

"But weren't you bitter thinking that the Oakland fire and Grandpa's move to San Leandro caused his murder?"

"I was bitter, but in law school we learned the difference between a *but for* cause and a *proximate cause*. If I take five minutes to have a cup of coffee and then get in a car accident I could say that *but for* the coffee the accident wouldn't have happened. But the proximate cause of the accident would be driver negligence-mine or the other guy's. It's the same with the house at Tahoe. *But for* that house I wouldn't have lost my practice. But the proximate cause was not the house-it was me. I spent too much time there and lost my clients because of it."

"So what about the criticisms you used to have about organized religion?"

"I'm still a critic, especially about dogmas that run contrary to my intellect. As a Catholic I'm disgusted about abuses by priests we hear in the news today. And I'm sorry to see the church turning more to the right. I hope it won't be like your evangelical crowd. But I'm starting to think that religion should be put back into my life, as it once was. When religion turned to violence it hit bottom. The violence of 9-11! The suicide bombings! How religion can lead a believer to kill is beyond my understanding of religion. But, for me, I go to church and feel good about knowing there still are priests like Leo and John. Did you notice at our Mass how they got along-Leo-a Creole from Louisiana and John-an Irishman from San Francisco? I guess I'll always be a critic, but I'm also encouraged when I see so many devoted and friendly people at church. I especially like to see the families with kids there."

"Do I hear you say that you're regaining the theology you were taught in Catholic school?"

"It may be more like the theology I came across in studying French."

"What was that?"

"The French call it *Le pari de Pascal*. Pascal said his belief in God was like a bet: *Si vous gagnez, vous gagnez tout; si vous perdez, vous ne perdez rien*." So I'm with him-I'll bet that God exists. Right now I don't need any more theology than that."

"Dad, has someone come along to cheer you up?"

"No shrink, if that's what you mean. You know I don't believe in them."

"What is it, then?"

"For years now Mom has been grieving over the fact that I sold Eva. Remember when you were a kid-you took a lava rock form the volcano in Hawaii-then you heard the legend that Madame Pele would give you bad luck until the rock was returned. You ran back to return it. Well, that's been happening to me. I've had Eva's curse for selling her.

"You've had bad luck because you sold Eva and she put a curse on you?"

"Yes, for 10 years now."

"Dad! I thought you were Mr. Cynic. What are you now-seventy three?"

"Seventy four."

"And you believe a legend like that?"

"I did. But now I'm starting to admit that what I thought was a curse was my excuse to find a scapegoat. Maybe, instead of the curse, I was the one to blame. And, you know, maybe Eva has forgiven me."

"Why would she now forgive you?"

"It could be that now she's happy again. It could be that now she's owned by a great composer who appreciates her and is willing to share her with others. And, I've found a substitute for her."

"OK, Dad. Whatever works for you. Now, what's the substitute?"

"Unbelievable! I saw it advertised on line. It's smaller with less carving, but it's a reproduction of Eva and it looks new."

"How much did that cost?"

"Now remember, Mom doesn't know about this yet. I want it to be a surprise. It was only $8,000. I don't have to sell the Steinway to get it."

"Have you paid that?"

"I have-plus $1,500 for shipping."

"How do you keep that from Mom?"

"I have a fund of money from my mother's estate-it's mine to manage. The new Eva will be my anniversary present to her."

"When will she know about it?"

"It's been shipped-from London. It should arrive in a few weeks. I'll have to plan how I'll show it to her."

"You said Mom's been grieving over Eva. Do you think this new Eva will solve her problem?"

"I hope so. Maybe it won't solve it completely but I hope it will stop her dwelling on it. I've also arranged to take her on a Mediterranean cruise. She doesn't know about that yet either."

"And how's your health? You seem to be in good shape."

"I'm feeling fine, especially now that I'm working out again."

"And what about your piano? I know you've had a bout with arthritis. How's that?"

"The arthritis isn't getting better, but what I do about it is. I'm starting to re-arrange music for less thumb activity, I'm getting back to playing with other instruments and maybe I'll be doing some solo playing around town."

"I hope, Dad, for your sake, that you're not just doing a lot of wishful thinking."

"Jeffrey, when you approach my age you'll realize that wishful thinking is the best thing we could ever do. Maybe, it's what your evangelical friends call prayer. And you know, I told you how I like to see the kids in church. I still picture you and Greg as kids. You're not one anymore, but I still love you."

"Thanks, Dad, for saying that. I love you too.So what about Tahoe? Are you enjoying that more?"

"Mom has agreed that we should sell it eventually. Now, we're just going to enjoy it. I hope you will too. Don't get the idea that I've become some kind of religious fanatic, but things are looking up."

"I've never thought of you as a fanatic. Let's say that, sometimes, not always, you're a little bit religious. And, it seems to me, you're happier that way."

"You may be right. After all, we have her back, or, we soon will."

"Her?"

"Yep! Our Nude Sleeping in a Hammock."

EPILOGUE-EVITA

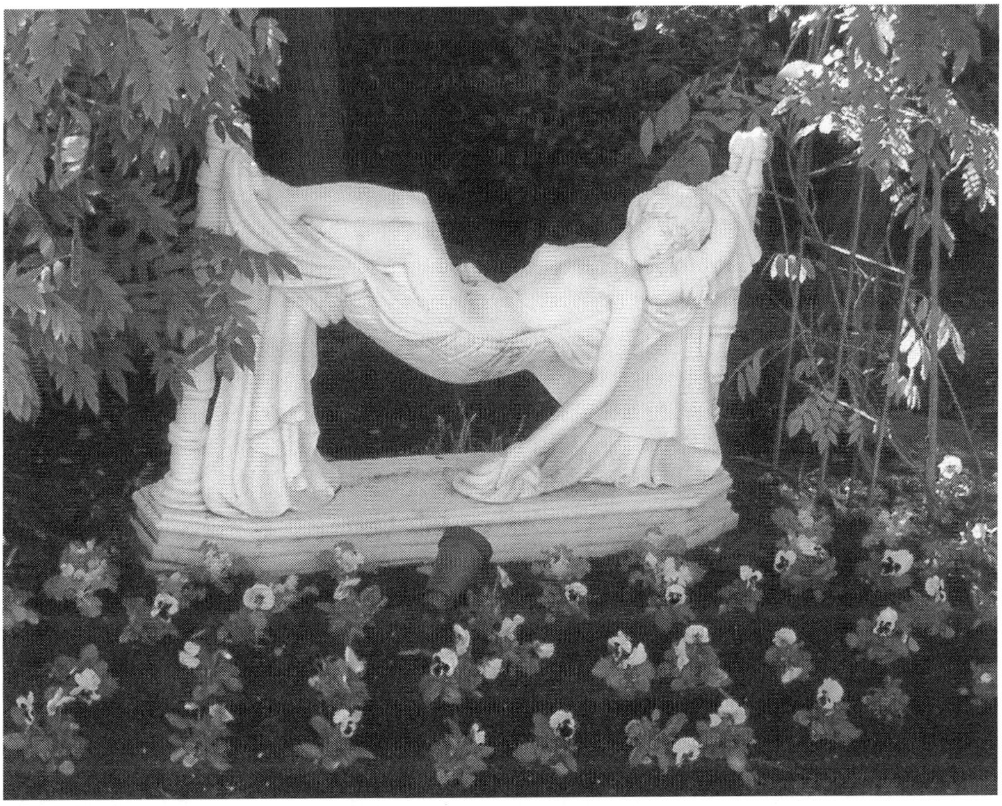

Berceuse, Chopin, Opus 57

28697334R00073

Made in the USA
Lexington, KY
30 December 2013